I0574974

# The Craft of Love
# by EE Ottoman

*Thanks to Kay Bashe for coming up with the title.*

*And thank you to M. for listening.*

The Craft of Love: EE Ottoman
First addition ebook copyright © October 19th 2018 by EE
Ottoman
Paperback copyright © October 7th 2025 by EE Ottoman
Credits: Cover by: Ashley Wong
Edited by: Jessica Cale and Marie Sager
All rights reserved.
Paperback ISBN: 979-8-9991883-3-5

This is a work of fiction. Names, characters, places, events, and incidents are either the product of the author's imagina-tion or within the public domain. Any resemblance to actual events or persons, living or dead, is a coincidence

EE Ottoman Original believes in copyright as a way of safeguarding the labor of artists, intellectuals, and creators. No portion of this book may be reprinted, including by electronic or mechanical means, or in any information storage and retrieval systems, without express written permission from the author, except for the use of brief quotations for the purpose of review.

NO AI TRAINING: Without limiting the author's exclusive rights under copyright, any use of this publication to "train" generative artificial intelligence (AI) technologies to generate text is expressly prohibited. The author reserves all rights to license uses of this work for generative AI training and development of machine learning language models.

## Content Notes

A note on the gender identity of the characters: This book de-picts a romance between a transgender man and a cisgender woman. Due to the historical setting, however, this is not the language these characters use for themselves.

Content warning: this book contains a brief discussion of past transphobia aimed at a trans child and gender dysphoria that could potentially trigger certain audiences.

# Chapter 1

*New York City*
*1831*

He'd been in search of a fresh tablecloth when he found the dresses at the bottom of one of the linen chests.

Today was market day, and Benjamin, who had been confined to the house while he recovered from a bad winter's cough, had offered to go with Georgiana. She'd declined and left Eli with Benjamin instead.

Benjamin didn't mind watching the baby, but he would have liked being able to go for a walk. Still, as Georgiana had pointed out, the cold morning air was probably not good for his still-healing lungs.

"What shall we do?" Benjamin asked Eli when they were alone, Eli perched securely on Benjamin's hip. Eli stared at him with large dark eyes and waved one slightly sodden fist in the air.

Benjamin carried Eli into the parlor, put him on the floor, divested himself of his coat, and got down on the floor as well.

Eli could do three things very well. One was putting his head up, craning his neck as he looked around him. He could also squirm around quite well on his belly, and the third was putting things into his mouth. Benjamin tried to encourage the last activity to only involve the wooden rattle he'd taken from Eli's cradle in the kitchen.

Together they happily passed the time by playing a game where Benjamin placed the rattle on the floor and Eli squirmed forward the few inches to claim his prize, Benjamin enthusiastically cheering him on.

Eventually, Eli's eyelids began to droop. Benjamin scooped him up and rocked him, singing softly until Eli drifted off, his small face pressed against Benjamin's shoulder. He roused somewhat and fussed when Benjamin laid him down in his cradle but settled again when Benjamin rocked it and continued his gentle singing. When Eli was well and truly asleep, Benjamin carefully snuck away to go about his own business.

Not that he had very much of that. There was the morning paper, which he read before carefully noting the weather in his diary. Timothy had brought notes on several of the shop's newest commissions back home with him the night before. "You could sketch out some ideas," he'd said. "I know I'd appreciate the guidance, as I'm sure would the boys."

It was hard, though, to sit and think through a piece, to plan it out and draw it knowing he could not go back to the shop. He wouldn't be the one beating out and molding the silver, wouldn't be overseeing one of the other apprentices cast the embellishments. He wouldn't be the one inspecting the piece, making changes to the design as he saw how it would come together into a whole.

He rose from his writing desk and fetched the broom. He swept out the main rooms of the house and halls, careful not to wake Eli. Then he went to find a fresh linen tablecloth so he could set the table for supper.

Georgiana kept such things in her linen chests instead of the closet to discourage insects from nesting in them. Benjamin knelt in front of the chest and was shifting piles of carefully folded white cloth when he caught a glimpse of pale pink. He paused, then dug farther into the chest.

There was pink there, fine pink linen with white flowers embroidered across it. Benjamin shifted the other items off of the cloth until he could see that it was a dress folded neatly at the bottom of the chest. Benjamin reached down, running his fingers against the cloth and the fine needlepoint before easing it out of the chest. There was another dress folded underneath it, plainer but still beautiful in a light blue cloth.

Benjamin didn't need to wonder who had made the dresses; the painstaking flower pattern had been one of their mother's favorites. These dresses weren't the right size for Georgiana to wear, though.

The back door opened and shut; it was probably Georgiana and the others back from the market.

"Benjamin?" Georgiana called, and there was the tap of her boots against the floor. "What are you doing down there?"

"I was looking for a tablecloth and I found these." He looked up from the dresses on the floor in front of him.

Georgiana was quiet for a long moment, her gaze also fixed on the dresses with their careful embroidery.

"Mother made them, didn't she?" It wasn't really a question, but Georgiana nodded anyway. "And they're not your size."

They were quiet, both looking down, not meeting each other's eyes.

"She made them for me." Benjamin reached out and smoothed one hand against the cloth again. He took a long, deep breath.

Beside him, Georgiana sighed. "I told her not to. I told her to make something for me if she wanted, or herself. It was such fine cloth, but she insisted. After she passed, I didn't know what to do with them. Maybe when Charity gets older, I'll be able to refit them for her."

Benjamin nodded, his fingers still tracing out the tiny flowers. He felt the thread catch, a tiny bit, on the calluses on his hands. "Why didn't you tell me?"

"I didn't want to upset you or make you feel guilty. I know it was difficult with mother and you. She was sick at that point, and I . . ." Georgiana shifted Eli, holding him tighter against her breast. "I should have told you. I'm sorry."

"No, I understand. But it must have cost her so much for the cloth and thread." Not to mention the hours upon hours of work.

They both looked back down at the flower dress in his hands.

"I think she intended for you to be married in that one." Georgiana reached down to caress the pink cloth. "Or at least hoped."

Benjamin's breath caught. He jerked his hand back as if the cloth might burn him. Pushing himself to his feet, he turned away from the clothes scattered across the floor.

Georgiana still knelt beside him. "I'm sorry. This is one of the reasons I didn't tell you," she said, and he heard the rustle of skirts as she stood.

"It's all right." The words felt heavy and wooden in his mouth. It wasn't all right, not really, but it was also not Georgiana's fault and never had been. She'd loved them both, him and their mother, and had tried to support and protect both of them.

He took a breath and squared his shoulders, trying to put the bewildering hurt aside. "Should I help you unpack the shopping from the market?"

Georgiana nodded, then gathered up her skirts and headed for the kitchen without waiting to see if he'd follow. After one last glance at the dresses on the floor, Benjamin did.

~*~

He couldn't stop thinking about the dresses.

After they'd eaten and done the washing up from supper, Georgiana had packed them away, back into the chest.

Still, those delicate embroidered flowers stayed in the back of his mind as he helped Georgiana with the house and children. They were there as he listened to Timothy recount the work of the shop, and when he sat down the next day to begin drafting plans for the teapot Timothy had brought him the commission for. He found himself sketching them into the handle and around the lip at the top of the pot before he sat back with a sigh.

He kept remembering the curve of his mother's back as she leaned over the sewing spread out across the table. The way her hands had moved over her work, quick and rhythmic, the needle catching the sunlight over and over.

He remembered standing in a dress she had made him.

Up until then, he'd worn girls' dresses, functional ones for work and play. This particular dress, though, had been a woman's dress—meant to be seen, to be worn to church or to a party.

When he thought of the dress now, it came to him only in snatches of sensation. The rustling noise it had made when he'd picked it up and put it on. The way it had felt against his hips, waist, and chest. The texture of the cloth against his skin. The dead, sinking weight in his stomach, every breath catching in his throat like a jagged piece of something he hadn't quite been able to swallow.

His mother's hands had rested on his shoulders for a moment and then run down to smooth the dress and shake out the skirt.

"There," she'd said, voice full of pride and satisfaction. "Don't you look pretty?"

He shouldn't have. He should have looked grotesques and wrong, unmatching pieces grating against each other. Her smile should have slipped from her face when she'd seen him.

It didn't, of course. Her smile stayed in place; her hands were warm on his shoulders.

Because he did look very pretty.

That had been the worst part, the betrayal that made tears start at the back of his eyes and his throat close up in sheer grief. Because his entire being had turned against him in that moment, showing the world a pretty girl in a new dress her mother had made for her.

Not the disaster happening underneath.

He hadn't cried then. He hadn't cried when they'd gone to church or when his mother's friends had fussed over him, telling him how lovely he looked.

He hadn't cried until that night, in bed with his hands pressed over his mouth. Then he'd *sobbed* with grief and sheer helpless rage as Georgiana lay stiff and silent beside him, not knowing what to say.

Benjamin stood up from his desk and put his writing things and the sketches away before going to find Georgiana.

She was in the kitchen kneading dough for bread while Charity sifted flour. Eli was beside them in his cradle, and Benjamin scooped him up in his arms and carried him to the kitchen window. It looked out onto the back courtyard where, their maid, Aveline, was currently bent over a washtub. Beyond her, Benjamin could see the silversmithy.

"You want to be there, I know," Georgiana said from behind him.

"Timothy is an excellent silversmith, and he has the boys to help him." Benjamin listened to the rhythmic thump of the dough against the top of the kitchen table, the soft noises Eli made as he sucked on his fist. "But of course I do. I want to be working."

He'd been away from the shop too long over the winter, sick in bed for weeks and then plagued by this cough that wouldn't seem to leave him.

Eli's small fist connected wetly with the side of Benjamin's head. Benjamin reached up and took Eli's hand loosely in his own, turning his head to smile at the baby and sticking his tongue out in order to make Eli smile. Eli just responded with a slightly worried look, so Benjamin let go of his hand and tickled Eli's chubby little side until he won a real smile for his trouble.

"I've been thinking about the dress mother made," he said, keeping his gaze on Eli's smiling face. "Are you really planning on refitting them for Charity to wear?"

By the time Charity was old enough to fit into an adult-size dress, the cloth would be thinning with age.

"Is there something you would rather I do with them?" Georgiana asked.

Benjamin didn't answer, bouncing Eli on his hip as he thought. Eli wrapped his fists around the top edge of Benjamin's waistcoat and made happy cooing noises into his ear.

Unbidden, another memory of his mother came to him. Sitting on her lap as a small child, watching her hands move across what seemed like a vast expanse of cloth as she carefully fit and arranged pieces on top. A warm memory, not tinged by grief or anger for once. He snatched at it without giving himself time to question or think it through.

"It would be a shame to waste the fabric," he said. "Perhaps they could be made into something like a quilt."

"Well, if you would like. The dresses are yours," Georgiana said, sounding dubious. "But I don't know anything about quilting. Do you really want to pay the money to commission it out?"

"I have some money saved, or I could trade for it," Benjamin said. Truthfully, he hadn't thought that seriously about it until now.

Georgiana finished kneading and patted the loaf out before placing it into the bowl at her elbow and covering it with a cloth. "I won't stop you. Just as long as any of the money you spend on it, whether commissioned or otherwise, doesn't come out of the household accounts."

"I wouldn't dream of taking it from there." Benjamin bounced Eli a bit more before going to retrieve of one his toys from the cradle.

Honestly, he wasn't even sure he'd get beyond drafting some ideas. It had been years since he'd put needle to cloth, and a quilt was a very large project to embark on. Still, it would give him something to think about that wasn't the shop and the work he could be doing there. Perhaps he could incorporate some of the designs into a silver piece, later on, so even if he never sewed the thing, the mental effort wouldn't go to waste.

Georgiana took the bowl of flour Charity had been sifting over and over until it was fine and began preparing the ingredients for the cake she would make next.

Benjamin carried Eli into the parlor and settled him on the floor.

The images of designs didn't stop playing in his head, unraveling themselves into the image of a quilt.

# Chapter 2

Remembrance knocked smartly on the front door of the house and tried not to glare at the cast-iron knocker while she waited for an answer. There was a small knot of worry at the bottom of her stomach. She wished she didn't have to take this time away from her workshop, and there was also the worry that she might not be able to find what she needed at all.

"May I speak with Mrs. Fleming?" she asked when a girl in a plain dress and clean apron answered the door.

"Of course." The girl moved back in order to allow Remembrance to step into the front hall, then disappeared farther into the house. It was a neat hall with white walls and a carefully swept floor. Some coats, hats, and a bonnet hung in an orderly row on pegs by the door.

After only a moment's wait, Mrs. Fleming appeared, tall and dark haired in a simple but respectable dress. A young girl of maybe five or six trailed along behind her.

"Mrs. Fleming, I hope you remember me. I believe Mrs. Whitlow introduced us previously. I am Miss Quincy."

"Of course. I am acquainted with your work, Miss Quincy, and am pleased to see you again." Mrs. Fleming nodded to Remembrance, then gestured to the child. "This is my daughter, Charity."

"Hello, Miss Fleming." Remembrance said as the little girl ducked out from behind her mother's skirts and gave Remembrance a tiny awkward curtsy.

"Come into the parlor," Mrs. Fleming said. "I'll have Aveline make us tea."

"This is not strictly a social call, but tea would be lovely." Remembrance tugged off her gloves and bonnet as she followed Mrs. Fleming through to the equally orderly parlor.

"So what is it if not a social call?" Mrs. Fleming asked once they'd settled and she had sent her daughter back to the kitchen.

"I have a business proposal to put to you. My supplier has recently proven to be unreliable." To put it extremely mildly. The swindling ass had been chronically unreliable and overcharged on top of that. Remembrance had put up with it for longer than she should have based on the convenience of being able to purchase all her materials from one merchant. That, however, was no longer worth the trouble he caused her. "I am looking for new ways to purchase the cloth and other materials. Mrs. Whitlow has told me you make very fine lace, and I was wondering if you would be willing to supply me with a few skeins as the need arises."

"I'm flattered my name was mentioned," Mrs. Fleming said. "How often do you think you will be in need of a few skeins of lace?"

"It's hard to say. I work on commission, as you know. The ladies who hire me usually make the decision if they would like lace included, although a lace edge is being more fashionable. I would, of course, contact you as soon as the commission came in to give you time to make the lace if you didn't have it on hand."

Mrs. Fleming regarded Remembrance keenly for a moment. "But it wouldn't be regular work."

"Well, I will admit I don't use lace as much as dressmakers or seamstresses do." Remembrance wondered if Mrs. Fleming had other clients. She probably did; she might even have enough craftswomen in need of lace that she could afford to turn occasional work down. If Mrs. Fleming wouldn't provide her with lace, Remembrance frankly didn't know who she would go to. Having to continue to search for a supplier and perhaps even lose clients over it was such an exhausting risk. For the hundredth time, she mentally cursed her ex-supplier.

"But I would be able to pay extra for lace," she said before she could talk herself out of making such an offer. "On account of it being by commission only, and because you will not have as much time to prepare the order as you might like."

A faint smile flickered across Mrs. Fleming's face. "Well, Miss Quincy, I think this arrangement could be quite advantageous for both of us."

"I'm glad you think so." Remembrance smiled as she mentally crossed one supplier off her list. A small extra fee would be worth it to know she would be able to acquire her lace from a reliable source. Besides, now that she was paying extra, she'd be able to make sure the lace Mrs. Fleming made for her was to her individual commissions' exact specifications. Now if only today's other meetings would go as satisfactorily, she could be back to work tomorrow without needing to worry about where her cloth and thread would come from.

"Georgiana, I—"

Both she and Mrs. Fleming turned at the sound of the voice.

There was a man standing in the doorway, holding a fat-cheeked baby in his arms.

Both she and Mrs. Fleming rose at the sight of him.

"I'm sorry. I seem to be intruding," he said.

Mrs. Fleming waved that off. "Nonsense. Benjamin, come in and meet Miss Quincy. Miss Quincy, this is my brother, Mr. Benjamin Lewis."

He was tall like his sister and dark haired like her too, with the same strong features, sharp nose, and keen gaze. He was also without a coat, his hair slightly rumpled where the baby had obviously grabbed several handfuls.

"I am pleased to meet you, Mr. Lewis." Remembrance gave him a small curtsy.

"Likewise, Miss Quincy." He tried to bow around the child in his arms, which ended up being a very silly thing to witness.

Remembrance bit back a smile.

"Ah, tea," Mrs. Fleming said as the maid came in behind Mr. Lewis with the child, Charity, trailing behind her.

There were a few moments of shuffling as Mrs. Fleming took the tray bearing the tea set. The maid took the baby from Mr. Lewis despite his protests and herded both children out of the room.

She returned a few moments later with an extra teacup for Mr. Lewis, who seated himself beside his sister.

"Miss Quincy and I have been discussing me providing her with lace," Mrs. Fleming said as she poured tea for all of them into the fine, if slightly old-fashioned, china cups. "Miss Quincy is a quiltmaker, one of the finest in the city, in fact."

Inexplicably, Mr. Lewis reddened at that. "Ah." He reached for his cup. "Well, the lace you make is very fine." He glanced at Remembrance and then away, taking a sip of his tea.

"Indeed," Remembrance said as Mrs. Fleming looked pleased with all the praise.

"What sort of quilting do you do?" Mr. Lewis asked, glancing at her again.

"All sorts. Although wedding quilts have been popular for a long time and still are," Remembrance said delicately. "What do you do, Mr. Lewis?"

"I'm a silversmith. I often work on commission."

Remembrance's gaze went to the silver teapot on the table, then back to Mr. Lewis. "That sounds fascinating."

He smiled a little at that.

"We do many small jobs but also commissions for larger pieces." He nodded to the tea set she'd been looking at. "Teapots and dinner sets are becoming more common. With more factories opening up and more bankers and merchants making the city their home, there is increasingly more work to be had."

"Yes." Remembrance thought of the daughters and wives of merchants, bankers, and factory owners, all of them eager to have fine needlework items but without the inclination or the skill to do the work themselves.

"Yes, I suppose you would know, us being colleagues of a sort."

She blinked, caught off guard for a moment. She'd never had a man describe her as a colleague before. She'd very rarely met one willing to admit what she did was work at all, in fact, much less the sort of skilled craftsmanship a silversmith must do.

Her own lips curved up into a smile, and Mr. Lewis smiled back.

Mrs. Fleming spoke up then, turning the conversation to lighter things like the weather and a few mutual acquaintances.

Mr. Lewis drank his tea and stayed quiet beside his sister, letting her fill up the space for the both of them.

When her teacup was empty, Remembrance rose. "Thank you, Mrs. Fleming, for your hospitality and for agreeing to my proposal."

"You are very welcome. Thank you for bringing me your business." Mrs. Fleming offered her hand, and Remembrance did not hesitate to shake it.

"May I see you out?" Mr. Lewis asked.

Remembrance nodded, already reaching for her bonnet. "If you'd like." Remembrance wondered why he would want to. Perhaps he was simply being polite. She eyed him interestedly as they stepped out into the hall.

"I have a business proposal of my own, I think," Mr. Lewis said. "I would like to seek your professional council."

"About quilting?" Remembrance asked dubiously, trying to imagine what kind of quilting or sewing advice Mr. Lewis could possibly want. It had not escaped her notice he'd said *he* wanted her council, not his sister.

Mr. Lewis hesitated for a moment, then nodded. "Yes. It's only a small project, but as you are skilled in this and I am not, your guidance would be useful, I think."

"In that case, come by Thursday morning if that time is convenient, and we can discuss your project then," Remembrance said, more than a little intrigued. She removed one of her cards from her purse and handed it over.

"Thank you." He took her card and considered it seriously before turning his gaze back on her. "Thursday morning will work well. Shall we say nine?"

"That would be suitable." He'd more than piqued her interest. She would have liked to have stayed and asked him for specifics about this mystery project of his, but she was very aware that she'd already made an appointment to talk about thread supply with Mrs. Cunningham over the noon meal. She would have to hurry as it was.

"If you will excuse me, Mr. Lewis, I'll see you on Thursday."

He opened the front door for her, then stepped aside, allowing her to sweep by him out onto the street.

~*~

Remembrance would be lying if she said she wasn't so very curious about what exactly Mr. Lewis had to propose to her. Gentlemen or men in general rarely came to her with commissions. Ladies brought commissions, design ideas, cloth they wanted to be incorporated, and specifications for what they wanted done, sometimes right down to the type of thread they wished her to use. While the money for such pieces almost always came out of a gentleman's pockets, they themselves hardly ever darkened her doorstep.

But this project seemed to be Mr. Lewis's and his alone.

It was curious enough that it stayed in her mind over the next few days.

Maybe Mr. Lewis was interested in commissioning a wedding quilt for a fiancée who did not have the means to commission one herself. Perhaps he meant it as a surprise for their new life together. That would fit with the gentle attentiveness he'd demonstrated when they'd met.

But maybe his business was something different altogether.

Of the three girls she employed, she chose Betty to be with her when Mr. Lewis called.

As she did before any client meeting, she made sure the parlor was spotlessly clean. Betty was dressed in a plain but neat dark dress with embroidery she had done herself at the cuffs and collar. It was one of Remembrance's stipulations that all the girls who worked for her dressed well and did their hair up, particularly on the days that clients called. If a girl could not afford a clean, well-made dress, Remembrance had one made for her.

The cost was a business investment after all. Remembrance had learned early on that a woman's professionalism and skill was judged on the cleanliness of her parlor and the neatness of her dress.

The dress she had chosen for herself was dark red with a hint of lace at the collar and a matching wide red belt with a buckle. She had hesitated over the belt when she'd dressed that morning, not sure it would be in poor taste to wear another silversmith's work, but it was the only belt she had that went. She'd pulled her hair back and secured it a twist at the back of her head, making sure her spectacles were straight and the glass clean.

Perhaps she'd spent more time getting ready that morning than was strictly necessary. He'd been kind and had treated her as if they were equals, and she didn't want him to think less of her upon their second meeting.

Her parlor was separated from the room where she and the girls worked by large double doors at one end. That way she could choose whether to have the doors open during meetings with potential clients, allowing them to see the workspace with its wide sunny windows, the quilt frames set up underneath, and the girls in their good dresses bent studiously over their work. Or she could choose to close the doors, giving the parlor a quieter, more intimate feel.

Today she chose to leave the doors open, trusting Mr. Lewis would appreciate the sight of her workspace, even as different as it must have been from his.

He arrived punctually at nine. Elizabeth let him in and showed him to the parlor, where Remembrance was waiting.

He was dressed, unlike last time, in a smart brown coat with a package tucked under one arm. He'd looked softly rumpled then, unassuming with a baby in his arms. Now he looked very much the respectable craftsman and business owner that he was. She found she preferred her first impression of him.

"Mr. Lewis." She smiled at him anyway and gestured to a seat across the table from her. "Please sit. Would you like coffee before we begin?"

"Yes, thank you." He sat in the seat she indicated, and Elizabeth moved silently to sit beside Remembrance.

She poured for the three of them, conscious that her coffeepot was neither as new nor as fine as Mrs. Fleming's tea service had been. She would not allow herself to become nervous, though; there was nothing wrong with her teapot. She sat back and regarded him as he drank his coffee.

"So, Mr. Lewis, how may I be of service?"

"Ah." Mr. Lewis set aside his cup and reached for the package he'd brought, undoing the string and folding the cloth aside to reveal the much finer fabric underneath.

He shook out first one and then another dress, lovely blue, and pink with what could have been taken for a print much like

Remembrance's own dress at a distance but was to her trained eye obviously embroidered. It was incredibly skilled work; she knew from experience how difficult it was to embroider like this, every flowering identical and evenly spaced. It would have taken someone—or more likely, a group of women—a long time to embroider the entire dress.

"My mother made these." Mr. Lewis's fingers moved carefully against the cloth, his hand smoothing it as he went. "I was hoping they could be made into a quilt."

*Ah.* "A remembrance quilt." Not as common as wedding quilts but still common enough if one was sentimental in that way. "It's not uncommon for gentlemen to have them made in order to remember a wife, sister, or mother."

He looked up at her, surprised for a moment, then strangely pleased, his mouth curving into a smile. He had a small dimple in one cheek that creased in when he smiled. It made him look younger, his face softer.

"What sort of design were you thinking of?" she asked, pulling her gaze away from it.

He pulled a folded piece of paper from his pocket and smoothed it out on the tabletop, beside the coffee service. There was writing across the back and a quite detailed drawing of a teapot from a number of different angles, but Remembrance didn't think that was what she was supposed to be looking at.

Instead, Mr. Lewis pointed to the sketches along the edges of the paper. "Something like this, maybe."

Remembrance leaned as far forward as she could, pushing her glasses up the bridge of her nose as she studied the design, taking in the twisting vines with acanthus leaves, bunches of grapes, and large detailed flowers. It was lush, naturalistic, and nostalgic in that it reminded her strongly of the designs she had grown up learning to sew rather than the softer, more romantically floral designs that were popular now.

"This would make a lovely whole-cloth quilt." She reached forward to delicately trace across one of the stylized leaves. "You will want it to be elegant, not garish or childish, and in appliqué, it will be harder. Especially given your limited color choices. Still not impossible." She considered the design for a moment, the quilt taking shape in her mind. "Make the body a white linen with most of the design traced out in stitching, but the blue and pink cloth used for the flower, perhaps, allowing them to bloom in color at certain intervals across the white. If you have or would be willing to purchase some green cloth, we could do some of the leaves as well. Perhaps the leaves closest to the flower's base. It would be unusual but striking."

She looked up to find him smiling again.

"That sounds lovely," he said. "I—" He broke off and looked away, his smile slipping. "It would mean a great deal to me to have a quilt like that."

*He must miss his mother; she must have meant a great deal to him.* She thought of her own mother, who came every Friday morning to sit and talk with her about her siblings and their families or listen to Remembrance talk about her latest commissions and the stories behind them over breakfast. She could not imagine life without her mother's strong, determined presence. For a moment, she had to fight the urge to reach out and comfort him in some way.

She did not, however. Instead, she said, "I would be happy to take on your commission."

He hesitated, his gaze flicking to the coffee service and then back to her. "Would you accept in payment in kind?"

She absolutely did not accept that, nor did she accept credit. Her clients paid her in full with real currency or they did not receive her services.

But she wouldn't lie to herself—she liked him, and the project looked fascinating to design, so she would break her rule this once.

She looked down at the beautiful drawing of the teapot and thought of the tea service Mrs. Fleming had used, one that had no doubt come from his shop. She could use a new service to have out when clients came.

"Very well, Mr. Lewis."

"Thank you. You will have to come by my shop and we can discuss your commission for me." He was beaming now, his eyes crinkling at the corners as if they were co-conspirators with some private joke. Colleagues again, she found herself smiling back, leaning toward him just a little, even though there was a table in the way.

"Then I will make an appointment to come by your shop."

"I look forward to it." He stood, obviously preparing to leave.

Remembrance did as well. "I will keep the dresses and these drawings if you don't mind," she said. "I will draw up a more detailed design for the overall quilt, which you will have the opportunity to approve, of course, before I begin work."

Mr. Lewis nodded and then paused, his gaze catching on her workroom, visible through the open doors, her worktables neatly organized. Lily and Samantha were bent over a quilt frame, currently occupied by her latest commission. He seemed quite arrested by the sight.

Remembrance gestured toward the room. "Would you like to see my workshop, Mr. Lewis?"

"Yes, please."

She led the way in, and he followed. Elizabeth stayed behind to refold the dresses and tidy up from the coffee.

Remembrance had a few smaller projects folded on the worktable, a set of embroidered handkerchiefs she was making for a soon-to-be bride, but Mr. Lewis's gaze was caught by the large quilt that Lily and Samantha were working on.

They both moved closer so they could see the pattern of a willow tree stitched in the center. Several complex borders of flowers and leaves encircled it, spreading out to the edges of the quilt. It was made of one solid piece of white linen, the pattern stitched, pale and delicate, in undyed thread. She watched his eyes widen and his lips part with obvious appreciation and something very close to wonder.

"This is a wedding quilt for the eldest daughter of a shipping company owner." Remembrance said, unable to hide her pride. "She chose a willow tree, the motif of her fiancé's family, I believe."

"It's beautiful." Mr. Lewis's hand moved as if he wanted to reach out and touch the pristine cloth, but he stopped himself halfway.

"Most of the wedding quilts I do are solid white like this one, but sometimes a bride will come with a yard of floral printed cloth from England or France she'd like me to incorporate." She did reach forward, passing her hand just above a patch of floral border she'd sewn herself. She didn't directly touch the fabric, though—white quilts needed to be touched as rarely as possible.

"Will that be similar to what you do with my quilt?" Mr. Lewis asked.

"Possibly. The technique of appliqué will be the same, but I will piece it together a little differently, I think."

His gaze went back to the quilt, tracing over the needle-work. "My mother used to make quilts like this. She was a seamstress, so she did not do a great deal of quilting or embroidery, but sometimes she would."

"Is the design you showed me one of hers?"

Mr. Lewis's expression became strangely closed and distant. "No." He didn't elaborate, and he looked so grave that she didn't want to pursue it.

When he did finally look back at her, he seemed to have shaken off some of the melancholy. "May I ask you something? I know this is an imposition, but I would so very much appreciate it if you could accommodate me. Would I be able to stop by your workshop from time to time once you've started working on the quilt? Just to see how it progresses."

She blinked. "Of course."

He'd looked as if he'd been expecting her to say no or be somehow affronted by the request. All of her clients stopped by regularly to check on her progress. If anything, she had ladies who hovered too much, steely-eyed mothers of the soon-to-be brides who wished to watch over her shoulder as she sewed every stitch, criticizing her every move although none of them would dream of lifting a hand to actually do the work themselves. She'd had to put her foot down on more than one occasion with such clients, but she couldn't imagine Mr. Lewis having the time or inclination to be that involved.

Truthfully, she would like to show her work to him again, watch his eyes light up over something she had made for him.

"You may stop by when you wish. Although if I am busy with another client, you may have to come back later."

"Of course." His gaze went to the quilt once more before he pulled it away with obvious effort. "Thank you so much, Miss Quincy."

"My pleasure." It was going to be a fascinating piece. It felt good to be making it for someone she liked, whose company she had found pleasant.

They went back to the parlor, and Mr. Lewis collected his hat.

"I hope to see you soon, Miss Quincy." He looked down at her, his gaze soft yet intensely focused as always. "Please call on me soon, and we will discuss what sort of service you would like me to make."

"I hope to see you soon as well, Mr. Lewis," Remembrance said and meant it.

# Chapter 3

It had been over a week since his last coughing spell, and his doctor had informed him that he could begin socializing again and might, if his health held, be able to go back to the shop over the next few weeks, although he should stick to light tasks and avoid long hours.

Given this, Benjamin decided to go on a small outing that evening. There was a lecture on New York State's natural flora hosted by the Botanical Club of Columbia University.

The lecture was hosted at a boarding house where most of the Botanical Club seemed to rent rooms. There were three papers being read that evening, with a light refreshment of biscuits and hot apple cider provided by the housekeeper.

The parlor was packed with attendees to the point where most of the men stood shoulder to shoulder along the edges of the rooms so the ladies and a few of the more elderly gentlemen could take the provided seats.

Benjamin stood against one wall, the men on either side of him so close he could barely move his arms. He listened to the first paper—on ferns and fungi found in the woodlands of the Hudson River Valley—while a cup of cider cooled between his hands. It wasn't exactly enthralling subject matter, at least not to Benjamin, but it was still nice to go out and be among people again. Maybe he'd be able to find a literary reading or a musical performance to attend next time.

There was a smattering of applause as the gentleman with the paper on ferns sat down and another gentleman with impressive sideburns and a paper that promised to be on indigenous species of trees stood to take his place. Benjamin's gaze drifted over the audience, catching on a pretty floral bonnet here and an embroidered shawl there.

His gaze caught on one figure in particular, her face turned attentively toward the speaker at the front of the room. At this distance and with this many people, Benjamin couldn't be sure, but he thought it was Miss Quincy. He felt a moment of relief at recognizing someone he knew, then curiosity rose to replace it. Was she particularly interested in trees, or, like him, had she simply chosen to be here out of a need for something social to do with her evening?

Her dark hair was pulled back from her face and twisted severely at the back of her neck as it had been the last two times they had met. She must have taken her bonnet off, unsurprising in the stiflingly warm room.

The lecturer, a Professor Bruster, had brought several large illustrated plates of trees and leaves, which caused murmurs of delight to travel through the audience as they were passed around. Benjamin watched as Miss Quincy took one of the illustrations from her neighbor, her dark head bending as she studied it. She looked away, down at something in her lap. He could not imagine what she was doing until he realized she must be taking notes of some kind on the lecture.

They were far enough apart and she was almost completely turned away from him, but he thought he could make out her brows furrowed in concentration as she listened to Professor Bruster and consulted her notes.

He wished he could be as engaged by it all as she was, but mostly he let the words wash over him. The lecture on trees ended, and a woman in severe black dress rose to give a lecture on botany for the amateur gardener, which mostly seemed to be an excuse for her to talk about the book she'd recently written on the subject. More murmurs of delight went through the assembled audience as she passed around a copy of her book so they could all admire the full-color illustrated plates of flowers contained within. Benjamin watched Miss Quincy bend seriously over the book, flipping through the pages.

His cider had gone the same temperature as the room, but Benjamin drank it anyway and waited for the lecture to come to an end. He wanted to speak with Miss Quincy, to ask her what had brought her out this evening.

The room applauded as the final speaker finished. Those that had been seated rose, and the room burst into chatter.

Benjamin pushed forward too, trying to make his way toward where she had risen from her chair. "Miss Quincy."

She smiled as she caught sight of him. "Mr. Lewis."

"Did you enjoy the lecture?" Despite his best efforts, he found himself closer to her than he might ordinarily have stood due to the press of people around them, although her voluminous skirts kept him somewhat at a distance. This close, he could see the small lines around her mouth and at the corners of her eyes, the indentations on her cheeks where her glasses rested. They were small, human imperfections in her formidable neatness.

"I did very much," she said, causing Benjamin to attend back to what she was saying. "But I am a Friend of the Botanical Club of Columbia University, so I go to all the lectures they hold."

"I'm not sure I know what it means to be a friend of the Botanical Club," Benjamin said, feeling at a loss. "This is the first botanical lecture I've been to."

"It's an off branch of the Botanical Club, which has an exclusive membership open only to botanists." Miss Quincy tucked her notebook away in the pocket of her dress. "Us Friends of the Botanical Club are more of a social group for amateur botanists and plant enthusiasts."

"And would you describe yourself as an amateur botanist or a plant enthusiast?"

She looked back up at him, her smile growing. "I'm not a botanist. I can't grow plants at all; I have no knack for it. But I enjoy reading and listening to people talk about botany, and I find studying plants and illustrations of plants helps with my design work. So I suppose I belong in the plant enthusiast category."

He nodded at that. "I can understand your reasoning; natural motifs are important in both our work."

Some people were still standing in small groups, deep in conversation, but many were heading for the door, ladies fitting bonnets back onto their heads and men sorting out where they'd left their walking sticks. Benjamin suppressed the urge to fiddle with the cuffs of his coat while he steeled himself to ask his next question.

"Do you plan on going back home after this?" he asked. "Or are you staying longer?"

"I was planning on going back home."

"May I accompany you? Just as far as your house." He held out his arm to her.

Her lips curved into a slight smile. "Aren't you worried what people might think?"

He laughed. "I hope both of our reputations are good enough to withstand a few blocks' walk, but if you'd rather not." He began to lower his arm, a tendril of uncertainty replacing his amusement.

"No, I'm sure you're right." She fit her bonnet onto her head, tied the strings under her chin, and took his arm.

Her touch was firm against the sleeve of his coat, firm enough for him to feel her hand through the layers of his clothing. He was more aware of her presence beside him now, the tiny movements of her shoulders as she breathed, the rustle of her skirts as she moved.

They managed to make their way through the front hall, choked as it was with people, and out into the evening air.

It was cool, but not unpleasantly so. The light breeze felt good against his face after the heat inside the house. Because this was New York, the streets were still teeming with people, even now with the sun starting to go down. Carts, carriages, and men on horseback went by on the streets while people on foot filled all of the rest of the available space. Most were going home after a day's work, but quite a few were going out to begin their nightly business. Some, like them, were enjoying an evening out.

Miss Quincy's hand remained firm on his arm as she wove her way through the crowds, avoiding puddles and other street debris with the ease of a native city dweller.

Benjamin did his best to keep stride with her. He rarely walked with anyone on his arm like this. He was very aware of her beside him, but also slightly, irrationally, afraid he might veer off course suddenly like a wayward ship and topple over her.

"So if you don't prefer botany lectures, what sorts of events do you attend?" she asked when they'd turned onto a slightly less crowded street mostly lined with houses instead of shops.

"I prefer more literary events, I suppose, rather than scientific ones," Benjamin said. "I sometimes go to musical performances, but I like literary readings best. I was lucky enough to hear Mr. Bryant read some of his poetry."

She tipped her head to the side. "I don't believe I have heard of him before."

That was a little bit hard for Benjamin to believe about one of the most celebrated poets in New York. He paused right there on the street, causing her to halt as well. Softly and faltering since he'd hardly memorized the entire poem, he recited, "'Vainly the fowler's eye might mark thy distant flight to do thee wrong, as darkly seen against the crimson sky, thy figure floats along.'"

Above them the sky was indeed crimson with the sunset. Thankfully, this street was less busy, although a few passersby did eye them with a mixture of curiosity and annoyance.

Benjamin cleared his throat, feeling his cheeks heat. "He is obviously of the more romantic persuasion."

"I had not heard that before. It's . . ." She seemed to search for a moment. "Very vivid."

Was she just being polite? It sounded as if she was. "Yes," he said, feeling crestfallen and slightly foolish.

Her hand pressed more firmly on his arm as they began walking again. "I meant it," she said with more conviction. "I don't have much experience with poetry, and I'm afraid I don't know how to appreciate it."

He smiled at that, feeling heartened. "I don't think there is any special way to appreciate poetry apart from if you like it or not or if it makes you feel a particular way. Perhaps if Mr. Bryant does another reading, we can both attend." Benjamin said before his courage failed him. "Even if you are not that taken with poetry, you might enjoy speaking with the man himself. He edits many different types of publications, you see, and is a great supporter of institutions of art and science here in New York. As you are."

She laughed at that, her mouth turning up in an amused smile as she considered him over the top of her spectacles. It made him feel very warm when she regarded him like that and very aware of her hand still firmly on his arm.

"I do try to support the sciences and other things I find interesting, and yes, I would gladly attend a reading of Mr. Bryant's work with you if the opportunity should arise."

His limbs felt lighter, his chest suddenly full with joy, and he couldn't help grinning back at her. "Then we shall."

They walked a little ways farther, neither hurrying. Benjamin watched Miss Quincy as she walked beside him, picking out small details to remember—the soft roundness of her face, the gentle brush of her dark eyelashes, the way her lips still turned up in a tiny smile. He wanted to hear her laugh again, to see her smile without restraint. He wanted to take all those smiles and laughter into himself until they became a part of who he was, until her amusement, her words, her very presence changed him, which was a ridiculously intimate thing to want from some he barely knew.

It was all very new, feeling like this. He'd liked her the few other times they'd spent in each other's company, but here and now he thought he might like her a great deal. Like he'd never liked anyone else before, in fact.

He looked away from her and cleared his throat before looking back and meeting her gaze this time. "So what other projects do you support aside from botany?"

She made a thoughtful noise, her gaze on him assessing. "I am also a dedicated supporter of the antislavery movement, particularly of the complete and immediate abolition of the institution. I do not wear nor do I sew with cotton cloth or cloth dyed with indigo, and I should warn you that I do not tolerate moderation on this issue. So if you support states' rights to self-determine, then you must tell me now because I am afraid we will never be able to speak again." She seemed quite serious, frowning up at him.

Benjamin blinked. "I believe in the antislavery movement, and I don't see how self-determination on the part of the southern states will ever lead to the end of that practice."

That seemed to satisfy her, and she nodded. "Also, from time to time, I attend a ladies' group on the welfare and uplift of destitute mothers. The group is run by my sister, you see, who is married to a pastor. I don't agree with much of the underlying thought to the group, so I don't attend often. I do hate quarreling with my sisters."

Given how strong her feelings on abolition were, he almost did not want to ask, but curiosity got the better of him. "What exactly do you disagree on?"

"That being destitute is a moral failing," she said, frowning gravely over the idea. "That families destroyed by the horrors of drink are somehow morally responsible for their position, which is, of course, nonsense. Do you know that here in New York, men who work on the docks and in the boatyard receive part of their pay in liquor?"

Benjamin shook his head.

"They are paid that way because the work they do is difficult and dangerous, but the bosses of the boat building and shipping companies have determined an inebriated man will take risks a sober man would not. Yet no one ever talks about the moral failings of our shipping company owners or lays the moral failing on the bankers and businessmen." Her tone was getting angrier and more passionate by the moment as she swept along, nearly alight with righteous fury. "Instead of hand-wringing over questions of moral failing, we should try paying these families enough so they can feed and clothe their children, and then decide where the failings lie."

"My," Benjamin said. "I can see why you and your sister argue if she is half as passionate about her side of things as you."

She stopped dead in her tracks, then rounded on him, her eyes flashing behind her spectacles. "Do you not think I am right?"

"Of course I think you're right," he said mildly. "Everyone should be paid for the work they do, and paid the worth of that work too. If the work is dirty or dangerous or requires great skill, they should be paid more. My apprentices do much of the casting work for my shop. They must tend the furnaces and handle metals that have been heated to the boiling point. I would never give them drink as a ploy to pay them less." Less than sober apprentices sounded like a nightmare. Benjamin spent enough time worrying that they would maim themselves terribly with the hot metal. Accidents like that were uncommon but still sometimes happened.

"I always try to pay everyone I employ fairly," he said as they started walking again. "My father died when I was young, and my mother carried on by herself after that. We were never destitute, but we—my sister and myself as well as my mother—had to work. If things had been different—if she had fallen ill sooner, I hadn't been able to secure an apprenticeship, or Georgiana had not been able to find work—we could have well been much worse off than we were, and it would not have been a moral failing on anyone's part."

"Exactly." Miss Quincy sighed. "The women in the group are not bad people, and they do good work. And there are quite a lot of destitute people who commit crimes and are deeply morally flawed, but their position has more to do with wealthy businessmen who do not treat their workers right and the fact that we do not have laws to force them to do so."

"Are you very political, then?" Benjamin asked her.

"I try to stay informed," Miss Quincy said. "Ah, here we are."

They had arrived, all too quickly, at the two-story stone house with brick chimneys where Miss Quincy lived and worked.

Benjamin came to a stop in front of the gate. "Thank you for talking with me and speaking so frankly about these sorts of subjects."

Miss Quincy let go of his arm, taking a step back but smiling at him. "Thank you for walking with me tonight, Mr. Lewis, for listening to all my opinions, and for discussing poetry. I enjoyed it."

"I would like to talk with you like this again. I know we have yet to meet to discuss the piece I am to make in repayment for the quilt. Perhaps you could come for tea on Saturday and we can discuss it then?"

As soon as the words were out of his mouth, he thought she would refuse him. She was thoughtful and passionate; surely there were more interesting people for her to spend time with.

She was already nodding. "I would like that."

His heart fluttered ridiculously at the words. "Then I will see you on Saturday."

"Saturday." She gave him one last smile, then pushed the gate open and stepped the few feet to the front door of the house.

He watched until the door had shut behind her, then turned to walk the few blocks back to his own home.

Above the rooftops and chimneys of New York City, the sky was still awash with golden light bleeding into deeper oranges and reds. A cool breeze pulled at the edges of his coat, bringing with it the faintest hint of salt and brine from the harbor. Benjamin tipped his head up to enjoy the full beauty of it as he walked, and he couldn't stop himself from smiling all the way back to his own front gate.

Georgiana was still up reading as he came into the familiar warmth and light of the house. Benjamin hung up his hat and strolled into the parlor, feeling very pleased with himself.

"How was the lecture? What you'd expected?" she asked, looking up at him.

"The lectures were fine, even if it turned out I'm not that interested in native varieties of trees." He settled himself down into a chair across from her. "I saw Miss Quincy at the lecture.

She allowed me to walk her back to her house, and we talked about a lot of things."

Georgiana watched him, her expression questioning.

"I think I like Miss Quincy very much," he said, his voice going soft over the words.

For another long moment, Georgiana searched his face, then her own lit with a bright smile. "Good. High time you had a companion."

A bit of his breathless happiness trickled away, replaced by a small hard knot in his stomach. He looked down at his hands.

"Don't overthink it," Georgiana said. "I can see you doing just that. Talk to her, Ben. Spend time together. If she wants something with you too, it's all well and good, but if she doesn't, move on. You're a good man; there will be others."

"I'm sure you're right," Benjamin said, even though anxiety still fluttered low in his stomach, tempering the better emotions there. He stood beside Georgiana, bent, and kissed her cheek.

"I want something like what you have with Timothy," Benjamin said, like a confession. He'd never said the words out loud before.

"Then court your lady, and be brave." She squeezed his hand one last time, then stood, closing her book and shaking out her skirt. "Now I'm off to bed. Goodnight, Benjamin."

"Goodnight."

He sat after she'd gone, thinking about the walk with Miss Quincy and what it might mean to be brave.

He sighed finally and stood. The knot of worry was still there inside him, but there was a lightness and a hopefulness there too.

# Chapter 4

He intended to court her.

She knew that, of course. The implications of their conversation had been quite clear, and more than that, it had been in the way he'd looked at her, in his voice, and the attentive way he listened. And she had agreed to allow him—no, she had agreed to be an equal part of this courting. She had taken his arm and felt her heart flutter, and when he'd asked to see her again, she'd wanted nothing more.

Remembrance took a deep breath.

She thought about the quiet way he listened to her, and the grave expression he'd often worn until that small smile would break through his serious demeanor, softening his face and bringing out that dimple. There was also the sweep of dark hair across his brow, his callused hands, and the strong solidness of his body. She could still remember the feel of his arm under her hand.

They were polite acquaintances, but the idea of becoming more hung before them now. It had just been so long since she'd known that sort of closeness with anyone.

She hadn't thought of Hope in a long time, but her thoughts turned toward her now. She thought about walking to the beach with her on a rare day off, arm in arm, the wind catching at the edges of their bonnets and pulling at their skirts. She remembered the way Hope had laughed, tipping her face close to Remembrance's own.

They'd eaten bread and cheese and fruit that Hope had brought, sitting on the rocky shore, watching the waves come in. They had been alone there, just the two of them, far from the business of the city. They'd taken off their boots and stockings and stood at the water's edge so the waves could lap at their feet. Hope had taken her bonnet off, and the wind had pulled at her hair, loosening tendrils from their braids and lifting them up around her face as she'd laughed and held her skirts out of the water.

Remembrance had thought Hope was the most beautiful thing in the world, and that she would never love anyone the way she had loved Hope in that moment.

She went to her chest of drawers and opened one, pulling out a small old wicker sewing box, the type of box just big enough to carry the things needed for some light mending or darning. Her first sewing box, given to her by her grandmother when Remembrance had been but a child.

She opened it and carefully emptied its contents onto the bed. At the bottom was a small collection of letters tied with soft pink ribbon beginning to fray at the ends. She tugged the ribbon off and opened one letter after another.

*My sweetest friend, my dearest companion, my Remembrance.*

Her fingers traced over the words.

*My beloved.*

*I have missed you so. I think of you always.*

She closed her eyes for a moment, then set the letters aside, burying her face in her hands. She wasn't sure she could do it again—care so much for one person knowing that it might not last.

What if Mr. Lewis took her hand and called her dearest, made her feel happy and cherished, then walked away and left her behind?

Would it be worth it, going through that again?

Should they not take that risk and remain as they were, pleasant acquaintances? She could fill her days with commissions, teaching her apprentices, and visits with her family.

She could go on like that and be happy and whole. There was nothing wrong with that life. But then she thought about his smile and the way he'd looked reciting poetry in the dusk.

When she thought of him as he had been the night he'd walked her home, it made her heart quicken. There was a sweetness to him, a gentle patience that made her want to make him smile, to say clever things that would make his eyes shine. When she remembered their walk together and his visit to her workshop, she couldn't help thinking of the movement of his strong hands, the shape of his mouth, and the long lines of his body. She wanted to see him relaxed and comfortable in shirtsleeves and with tousled hair, watch him play with his baby nephew, and hear him laugh.

She wanted it with a fierceness she hadn't felt in a very long time. Truth be told, she couldn't stop herself from caring about him, from going hot and thrilled and anxious all at once when she thought about him.

Maybe the risk would be worth it after all.

~*~

On Saturday she put on one of her favorite work dresses. It was a bright goldenrod yellow printed with a rust red pattern of flowers and leaves that were supposed to be imitation chintz. The dress was older, made from the first really good length of cloth she'd ever had enough of her own money to buy. It was plainly cut, but she still loved how the red and gold of the cloth brought out the subtle red in her own dark hair and the gray of her eyes. She wore her best shawl over it, knitted lace made out of a very fine thread of lamb's wool, which fancied up the outfit somewhat.

She'd made sure to clean and shine her boots the night before and was now as respectable as any other business owner in New York.

Notably more respectable than most.

It was a short walk between her house and the house Mr. Lewis shared with Mr. and Mrs. Fleming. Remembrance kept her pace brisk, weaving between people.

The silversmith shop owned by Mr. Lewis and Mr. Fleming sat just behind the house, facing the opposite street. Even though she was approaching from the back, she could still smell the smoke mixed with the strange acrid tang of the metals and a wet, earthy yet not quite natural scent she couldn't identify.

She knocked on the door only to have it pulled open a few seconds later by Mr. Lewis himself.

"Miss Quincy, please come in." He sounded as if he'd run—or at least walked very fast—to the door.

That made her smile. "Thank you, Mr. Lewis."

The table in the parlor had been laid with tea and Mrs. Fleming sat by her lace bench working on a piece that looked like a long, winding garland of flowers. She looked up and smiled at Remembrance but made no move to join them at the table.

Remembrance looked back at Mr. Lewis. She had never hesitated to speak with him before. His presence invited openness, at least from her, yet she was suddenly afraid she wouldn't say the right thing.

Mr. Lewis had gone tentative and the fact that he was obviously nervous too made her feel better.

"Would you like to sit?"

She sat, and he seated himself across from her, perched a little too close to the edge of his chair. She watched him pour for the both of them.

Once he set the teapot down, his hands settled awkwardly in his lap like he wasn't quite sure what to do with them. "So, do you have any plans or ideas for what kind of tea or coffee pot you might like?"

She considered, taking a sip of tea. "A teapot, perhaps, or do you think that would be too ostentatious? I would like to have something to use when I'm seeing clients, but ladies prefer to think that I am respectable while also being below them in every possible way." She gave him a sharp smile. "It would be inadvisable for them to think I have done just as well for myself as they have."

"Perhaps if the piece were plainer, it would serve your needs better. I know flourishes and flowers are becoming popular, but I could do something simpler and still make it elegant." He pulled a piece of paper and a pencil from a side table and leaned forward so he could lay the paper on the table between them. His pencil moved in quick, sure strokes across the surface of the page, detailing lines and shapes.

She watched the shape of a teapot with a rounded body and elegant curved spout take form under his hands. His strokes were confident, so sure was he of the design that must be coming together in his mind.

There was a pull in her own chest at that, a recognition of the process if not the method. She thought of the way designs would take form in her mind, drawn from older stitches and patterns she'd learned but always slightly different, unique to themselves and made alive by that.

The sketch of the teapot forming in front of her was much the same. She could see the shapes she remembered from tea services at the houses of her mother's friends when she'd been young. That plain republican style that had been more popular than was made softer and more modern under his hands.

"We can do some engraving if you want. A simple design around the top, maybe. I could even incorporate your maker's mark into the design. That's a very popular touch."

She stiffened across from him, feeling suddenly cold. "I don't have a maker's mark."

His pencil paused. He looked up at her, surprised. "You don't?"

"No." Her hands felt wooden as she adjusted her shawl. "My clients would not allow it. Having another woman's mark—an artisan's mark—would ruin the domestic fantasy that my clients made the pieces themselves."

When she'd told him about needing a plain tea service so her lady clients could go on thinking of her as below them, there had been a strange satisfaction in the admission. She was not below them, but she could play the part as any shrewd businesswoman would. This, though—this was an honor that had been taken away from her. Mr. Lewis no doubt marked every piece he made, a symbol of ownership and pride in his craft, as did nearly every other artisan in the city; even bakers marked their loaves with their own unique designs. Women who made butter to sell at the market molded it into a shape or pattern shapes that could be used by no one else. But Remembrance would never be able to use a mark of her own.

In order to save some rich women's pride, some of hers had to be taken instead.

She shouldn't care. She thought she'd gotten over this a long time ago. She was proud of her work, and those who needed to knew which pieces were hers.

Still, she pressed her lips together in a tight, straight line and didn't meet his eyes.

"Well." His tone was low and soothingly gentle without a hint of pity or dismay. "Do you have a pattern or motif that you work with often? Something that is distinctive to your work? We could use that instead."

She felt herself soften a bit at that and leaned forward again to study the page. "Here." She reached for the pencil he still held. Their fingers brushed, just for an instant, as he relinquished it to her. Awareness of him passed through her entire body, a sudden and urgent pressure from underneath her skin.

She swallowed hard and tried to think only of the design she wanted to draw and not of him, sitting quietly on the other side of the table. She could hear him breathing softly in the space between them. They weren't close enough that she could feel the heat of his skin or the solidness of his body, she knew that, but she could almost imagine it.

Her hand shook ever so slightly as she leaned over the paper. She struggled to lay aside her acute, totally distracting awareness of him and concentrate on what she was supposed to be drawing. She started with the leaves; that's where she always started, leaves—delicate yet strong, subtle and fresh, or lace thin and dry. Leaves spoke of life and thriving and change. They were each unique, imperfect, and complexly beautiful. She thought about leaves, and her hands moved across the paper, adding her designs to his.

In her own work, she'd sometimes stitch out leaves from actual plants. Some plants had particular significance to her clients, or they possessed symbolism that fit well within the overall piece. Other times, though, she'd make up the design, leaves that probably didn't exist on Earth, based on illustrations or art she'd seen, stories she'd been told, or half-forgotten imaginings from her childhood. She always saved her truly mythical or strange designs for her private, personal projects. These were plants that could never really exist outside the realm of fantasy, with all sorts of wild fruits and large lush flowers and, of course, leaves.

The pattern she drew now was very much like that, interlocking leaves from a tree that grew and existed only in her mind. Less fantastical, perhaps—more elegant and subdued to fit with Mr. Lewis's work, but hers nonetheless.

She looked up to find him watching her with a small pleased smile.

"That's beautiful." He leaned forward, bringing them much closer together. Her body tightened again with awareness of him. It would be easy for her to reach out and touch him now, to put a hand on his shoulder, his arm, or his hand as one hovered over the page, so very close to her own. She could feel her face heat and looked away, hoping he wouldn't notice.

If he did notice, he only asked, "What about continuing this pattern down the handle?"

She looked back at the sketch. "If it were a simpler variation, maybe. Otherwise, I would be afraid of it being too much."

"Whatever you prefer," he said easily, sitting back.

She made several attempts at simpler and stylized versions of the leaf pattern before shaking her head. "No, I think it will be better to just leave it plain."

Mr. Lewis nodded. "This should be enough for a start; do let me know if there are any other features you want." His gaze lifted to meet hers, almost shy. "Would you like to see the shop?"

She'd never been inside a smithy before. All the things she had that would have been made in such a place had been bought at shops or gifted to her. She was trepidatious at the potential noise, smell, and danger. It was so far removed from her own quiet sewing room. But she nodded firmly and rose. "Of course."

He stood and led her back out of the parlor and into the front hall. "I'm happy to show you, but we'll have to go out and around the house to get there. I hope you don't mind."

"Not at all." She pulled on her bonnet and gloves and followed him out of the house. They headed down the street, back the way she had come, and she realized he was going to lead her around the whole block so they would come out on the same side as the shop.

There must have been a quicker route, either cutting through the house itself or through an alley.

He was choosing to take her this longer way rather than expecting her to pick her way through a garbage-strewn alley. It was a futile gesture—she had been born and raised in the city, and neither alleyways nor garbage was new to her—but it was also sweet. Besides, she was wearing her favorite dress.

They turned the corner together, walking side by side but not quite touching. There was a smartly painted sign reading *Lewis and Fleming Silversmithing* hanging over the door of the shop. Remembrance regarded it appreciatively. She did not have a sign of her own since she rented her space, but she rather wished she could.

Mr. Lewis pushed open the door and led the way inside.

As soon as she stepped in after him, the noise and heat from the furnaces and forge hit her, along with the smell of metal and some harsher scent that pricked her nose right up into her head. She took several careful breaths to acclimatize herself to it, then carefully arranged her expression so as not to show any distaste or discomfort.

It was dimmer in the shop than the street, but her eyes adjusted enough to make out the workbenches set up along the edges of the room and a few in the center. One entire wall was covered in hammers of every imaginable size and shape. There were anvils on every workbench, most with rounded edges she assumed were to help mold the bodies of vessels. There were also wooden cups of long, fine metal instruments, some with rounded or blunted tips, others obviously meant for cutting and piercing. There were other pots with files and small, almost delicate-looking saws as well.

A boy sat closer to the door where they'd entered, polishing finished silver pieces with a rag. Remembrance's gaze was caught by the beautiful scalloped coffee pot in the boy's hands, tall and elegantly curved.

Toiling by the furnace and forge was a slightly older man stripped down to his shirt, the sleeves rolled to his shoulders. He was tending to various racks and crucibles of heating metal, pausing every so often to pump the bellows to keep the fire high.

Another young man bent over a wooden post with several shallow divots of different sizes carved into its top, into which he was beating metal with a small hammer. It took her a moment to realize he must be shaping the handle for some piece of silverware.

"We make a great many sets of spoons." Mr. Lewis's voice came close to her ear, most likely in order to be heard over the hammering. Still, she bit her lip, trying not to be aware of his closeness and failing completely. He was to her right and just behind, angling his body closer to hers so she could hear him when he spoke. This close, she could imagine the way his breath would feel against her ear, her hair, the slope of her neck. She took a very careful breath to steady herself.

She was caught off guard by the intensity of it. She'd thought about his physical presence before when she'd remembered the moments they'd shared together. In the privacy of her own bedroom, she'd been able to think about the shape of him, but this was still new, this sweet burning awareness of him and his proximity to her.

He moved away and stepped around her.

"Fleming."

A man hunched over a workbench turned and stood.

Mr. Fleming, she presumed, wiped his hands clean on a rag and came over to them. He looked to be about Mr. Lewis's age. He was taller, though, with dark blond curls sticking to his forehead and an easy smile.

"Fleming, this is Miss Quincy," Mr. Lewis said. "She is a quiltmaker over on Warren Street."

"A pleasure to meet you, Miss Quincy. My wife told me of your kind business arrangement with her." Mr. Fleming nodded to her, and she bobbed a tiny curtsy in return.

"It's my pleasure to do business with such a fine lacemaker as your wife." Remembrance told him, which made him smile in a charmingly boyish sort of way, so pleased and proud with her compliment to his wife's achievements. She could see why Mrs. Fleming liked him.

She smiled back at him, then turned to Mr. Lewis. "Where do you normally work when you are in the shop?"

"Oh." He looked startled that she would ask. "Wherever I am needed, I suppose. If I need a mold to stamp out a piece, I work there." He nodded to the boy making spoon handles. "But most of the time, at this workbench." He beckoned her to a wooden bench on the opposite side of the shop from where Mr. Fleming worked. It was a very neatly organized, immaculately clean space, all the tools carefully lined up or stored in their own cups.

"What are these for?" She reached out to lay the tips of her fingers against a funny round wooden handle attached to what looked like a slender knife blade. There were quite a few of them in different shapes and sizes hanging from a rack at the back of the worktable.

"A graver. I use it to carve the design into the metal for engraving. Please don't touch the blade; they're extremely sharp."

"I've never seen a graver before. Although, I suppose I vaguely knew how engraving happened." She gazed at the row of blades in front of her. "They are larger than I imagined. It must be very difficult to make such small yet complex designs."

"I suppose it's like anything—you learn to do it," Mr. Lewis said as she turned back to him. "And while the handles need to be large enough to fill the entire hand so that you can have a good strong grip, the tip of the blade where it actually cuts through the metal is very fine, which allows for more delicate work."

"Lewis is also being very modest." Mr. Fleming said coming over to join them. "Engraving is an extremely difficult skill even for seasoned metalsmiths, and Lewis's engraving is some of the best in the city."

Mr. Lewis went a pink at the praise, which Remembrance found endearing, but he also didn't deny it. Her estimation of his skill rose.

"Thank you for showing me this."

Mr. Lewis shook his head, but he was smiling. "I hope it wasn't too terribly dull."

"Not at all." She could not think of a word that suited the noise, smell, and constant activity of the workshop less than "dull."

"I'm so glad." Mr. Lewis said, taking a step closer to her again. He looked glad too, as if sharing this space with her and being able to speak to his process had truly pleased him.

She looked at him, his serious yet hopeful expression, the curve of his mouth, and the softness of his shoulders as he bent toward her. For all the clatter around them, his attention was on her and her alone. It made a warm, soft feeling bloom in her chest, spreading slowly outward, affection and a deeper, more tender emotion filling her up until she thought she might overflow with it.

She wanted to take his hand very badly.

His hand would be warm and rough against hers, and she would watch his eyes widen in surprise as she touched him.

She didn't, though. She just smiled and let him escort her back to the door.

They traversed the street back the way they'd come to Mr. Lewis's house. He was quiet as they walked, but the silence between them was not oppressive. Truthfully, Remembrance preferred quiet to chatter.

"So is there anything else I should keep in mind for your piece?" Mr. Lewis asked when they were back inside the house once again.

"I don't believe so. Thank you for taking it on."

"My pleasure, and it is in payment for your own work." Mr. Lewis said. "Truth be told, I'm excited about it. I was ill for most of the winter, which has kept me out of the shop almost entirely these past months. This will be the first commission I will have the chance to work on from start to finish since returning."

Remembrance's gaze rose to regard him sharply at the mention of his illness. She had found it strange that he had been at home that first day they had met. But if he had been ill, it would have explained it.

"I trust you are well now."

He smiled gently at her. "I am much better, thank you. And my doctor says there should be no lasting harm. It was merely a bad case of winter illness that lingered."

Some of the concern that had begun to slide coldly into her stomach left her. "I am glad to hear that."

They were still standing in the front hall of his house, acting so stiflingly polite toward each other, so careful and proper down to the correct amount of distance between them. She thought about her earlier desire to touch him, wondered what he would do if she stepped forward and closed the space between them.

She imagined the feel of his coat under her hands, the rise and fall of his chest, the way his lips would part. She would be able to see what his eyes looked like up close, their subtle shift of color. That close, she would be able to kiss him if he wanted her to.

It was . . . unsettlingly vulnerable, liking him like this.

It made her stomach knot up and her hands sweat. She felt suddenly small and unsure.

At the end of the day, she couldn't hide from the fact that they did not know each other very well; this separation between them was both infuriating and also rather a relief.

Let him court her with careful words and tea a little while longer before she was forced to decide.

"Thank you, Mr. Lewis. For the tea and showing your workshop to me." She forced a smile she no longer truly felt. "It was a very pleasant way to spend the afternoon."

*Pleasant.*

Pleasant was easy, vague, and not really what she wanted.

Still, she turned to the front door, tugged it open, and stepped out to the street.

"Miss Quincy."

She turned back toward him. He'd stepped out of the house and was standing a few paces behind her on the street.

"I . . ." He took a breath, then a step toward her. "It should be obvious that I like you very much, Miss Quincy, or at least I hope it's obvious . . ." he trailed off, sounding unsure, his gaze searching her face. "Either way, I want to be clear about it now so you don't mistake my intentions."

She hadn't mistaken his intentions, but she had hoped to postpone this moment. She took a breath of her own and stepped forward too. "What are your intentions, Mr. Lewis? Besides liking me?"

If he said "marriage," she wasn't sure she could do this. The idea of turning him down cold on the street made an awful twisting pain start in her gut, but she just couldn't . . .

"To court you," he said, his voice going low. "To know you better, and to share time and affection with you."

They were standing close now, closer than they had ever been.

She could feel the decision looming over her now, but she'd wanted more time and space to breathe. Part of her thought of Hope laughing on the beach, but a larger part was focused on him, on his closeness, the realness of him, and the small frown line beginning to form between his eyebrows as he watched her.

"Mr. Lewis." She reached out, her gloved hand falling to cover his. "I would like that, I would, but you have to understand that you are not the first to share my affections. The last time, when it ended, I was . . ." *Betrayed, alone, heartbroken.* She took another steadying breath. "I need time to understand this."

His fingers moved under hers to take her hand. Even through the layer of cloth that separated them, she could feel the firmness of his grip, the shape of his hand against hers.

"Do you not want to me to continue?" he asked, and she knew if she were to say "yes," he would stop. Then they would be mere business acquaintances with shared commissions and a careful, polite, *pleasant* cordiality between them. It would never grow to be more than that.

That thought sent a curl of panic through her. "No," she said, perhaps too quickly and too loudly because he blinked at her, taken aback. "No. I don't want us to stop, but go slowly maybe."

His mouth curved into a small smile. "All right. Slowly, then."

She smiled too, the panic giving way to relief.

"Can I . . ." He hesitated, his gaze still fixed on her face. "Walk you home? Would that be too fast?"

He was so serious and earnest as he said it. Her smile became wider, followed by laughter she couldn't contain. She pulled her hand free and pressed it against her mouth for a moment. "I'm sorry. I didn't mean to laugh at you, I just . . . yes, you may escort me home. Thank you for asking, Mr. Lewis." She dropped her hand and held out her arm to him.

He looped his arm through hers.

They walked together in easy silence. Remembrance's whole body hummed with his closeness and all the possibilities and anxieties of their position. She couldn't help glancing at him as they walked, taking in the long slender lines of his face, his dark hair and eyes, his hawkish nose, and the shape of his shoulders under his well-fitted coat. She thought about his dimple when he smiled and his hands when he drew, and she quivered all over again inside, her heart racing fast.

It was only a few blocks from his house to hers, but it felt much shorter than that.

# Chapter 5

Benjamin walked quicker than normal down the New York City streets, avoiding a large pothole filled with God only knew what with practiced ease.

Almost as soon as he'd returned home from escorting Miss Quincy, the doubts had set in. Had he pushed harder than he should have? Should he have not said anything at all and given them both longer to meet and talk before broaching the subject of more? Had she agreed to allow him to court her simply because he had put her on the spot?

He didn't like that thought at all, but he wasn't sure what to do about it.

Miss Quincy had talked about already having been in love once before, and Benjamin was very aware that he never had. If she had been courted by another, she would be far more knowledgeable about such things than him and more likely to realize it if he made a mistake.

He didn't want to make a mistake. The idea of her being hurt by him, even unknowingly, made his stomach knot. On a baser level, he did not want to appear clumsy in her eyes, young and inexperienced.

Even though he was, in fact, very inexperienced.

Benjamin sighed, staring up at the pale blue sky until a woman carrying a basket of laundry jostled him nearly off the sidewalk and into the street.

"Excuse me," Benjamin said to her apologetically while she glared at him.

"Look where you're going or you'll be pushed under a cart next time," she snapped before sweeping by him, followed by two young girls also carrying laundry baskets, who both gaped at him as they passed by.

Benjamin felt his cheeks heat under the weight of their curious stares.

That was another thing he had been trying not to think about, but it had kept him awake more nights than he cared to admit. He wasn't handsome by any stretch—more than that, there were parts of his appearance that would always simply be too feminine. He tried not to dwell on such things, but he wasn't unaware of the puzzled glances he sometimes received.

He looked down at himself. He was wearing one of his best coats, the gray one with the silver buttons he'd made himself, with matching gray trousers. Before coming here, he'd dressed carefully, washed, and put on a clean white shirt and neckcloth. Yet people still looked.

What if she didn't find him attractive or would come to resent the looks? There were so many other men she could be with, men who wouldn't get her looked twice at on the street.

Intellectually, he thought she would surely have said something if that were true and turned him down straightaway. That didn't stop the fear from shadowing his thoughts and telling him that perhaps she was just being kind while she thought of some excuse to get away from any further meetings. Or perhaps it was their business arrangement that kept her from sending him away.

That idea stopped him in his tracks even as the city moved around him. Horses pulling carts or omnibuses clattered by on the street. Men yelled to one another, children laughed and screamed, and he could hear the chatter of voices as a group of women in brightly patterned dressed pushed by him, giving him curious looks as they passed.

He shook his head firmly. *You are being ridiculous.* He quickened his pace again.

When they were together, it was easy. She was so elegant with such a sharp mind and a confidence that made her command any room she was in. He didn't have these thoughts then, swept away as he always was by the sheer joy of her presence. It wasn't until after, when he was alone, that the doubts would creep in.

Due to his pace he arrived at Miss Quincy's house sooner than he would have liked. A fully irrational sense of dread squeezed his chest as he rang the bell and waited for the landlady's maid to answer the door.

The maid showed him in, and Benjamin climbed the stairs to the rooms out of which Miss Quincy lived, worked, and attended to her clients.

He knocked and the door was pulled open a few moments later by Miss Quincy herself.

"Mr. Lewis." She sounded pleased enough to see him. She looked pleased to see him too, with a slight smile curving her mouth. It went a long way in soothing his nerves.

"Miss Quincy. You sent word that you had begun work on the quilt?"

He'd begun work in the shop again, doing ridiculously simple non-strenuous tasks but had taken these few hours in the late afternoon specifically to walk over to Miss Quincy's house once the message had come to him through Georgiana.

"Yes, in fact." Miss Quincy beckoned him through the empty sitting room to her workshop.

The pure white masterpiece had been removed, and an expanse of soft cream linen now stretched across the wooden quilting frame. Two of Miss Quincy's apprentices bent over it, stitching a border of interlocking leaves with undyed thread just a shade darker than the cloth itself.

Vines stretched from the border, although instead of a wild mass, they formed careful patterns, crossing, interlocking, and curving across the cloth. From them grew flowers and fruit cut from a cloth Benjamin recognized.

"It's beautiful," he breathed the words as he leaned closer to the cloth, trying to pick out the individual stitches with his gaze. Each stitch was so tiny and precise that from a distance, they were indistinguishable from each other. He reached out and traced them with just the tips of his fingers, feeling as much as seeing the fineness of the needlework.

"I'm glad you like it." With a soft rustle of skirts, Miss Quincy settled herself on one of the low benches that had been pulled up to the quilting frame. "It has been coming along quite nicely, I think." She let her hand skim across the stitch-worked border. "Many designs I stitch are softer and more organic than this, less geometric, but after seeing your workshop, I thought I might mirror some of your silverwork designs."

"I can see that." He was still hovering beside the quilting frame while the women sat.

Miss Quincy shifted over farther on the bench, then patted the space beside her. He hesitated for a moment, then sat.

"When we first started, I was afraid the pattern might not translate. Quilting and silversmithing are such different mediums." Miss Quincy picked up a needle that had been pinned carefully to the edge of the cloth.

"I think the pattern suits the quilt well," Benjamin said. "I can see how not all of the designs I use would translate, but this is magnificent."

She smiled at his praise, looking so pleased it made his heart beat faster.

"You must have loved your mother a great deal to want a quilt in her honor."

For a moment Benjamin was quiet, contemplating the quilt. He'd known the topic would arise eventually. It was natural for her to be curious, and she'd mentioned memory quilts when he'd first brought the dresses to her.

"Actually, the relationship between my mother and me was a difficult one." He kept his voice low enough for them to speak just between each other.

Her hands paused over the cloth. "Oh . . . I didn't think. I am sorry if you don't want it brought up."

"No, it's all right." His own hands traced the leaf pattern again. "This is part of why I wanted the quilt made." He was quiet for another long moment. "She loved me a great deal, you know. Doted on me, even. But I . . ." He swallowed, thinking about the years' worth of disappointment in her voice the last time they had spoken. "I tried very hard to be a dutiful son, but she would have preferred me to be made in her image in many ways."

"I see."

He met her gaze finally. Her eyes were very dark behind the lenses of her glasses. She was no longer smiling, but he thought she did understand him.

Suddenly, she turned from him to face her apprentices seated across from them. "Girls, I believe it is time for your noon break. Mr. Lewis and I must speak privately."

Her tone was clipped and firm, allowing for no argument. Both of the girls nodded and tidied their sewing kits away before standing.

"Should we set a place for you for the noon meal?" One, a pretty red-haired girl, asked as she stood. Her gaze flicked briefly toward Benjamin then away.

"Set two," Miss Quincy said firmly before Benjamin had a chance to make some sort of excuse for not staying.

The girl nodded and followed her companion out. Benjamin could hear them begin to talk among themselves in low voices as soon as they were out of the workshop.

"I shouldn't intrude on your meal."

Miss Quincy shook her head. "Nonsense. There's plenty for all of us. Unless you'd rather not dine here?"

"Well, if you're offering."

"Good." Her expression softened as she watched him. "I am truly sorry for bringing up something that is painful for you."

"It is painful but not unbearably so. It's been some years since she passed, longer before that since we had spoken to each other. I suppose I was hoping that this quilt would help me make something better from those memories. Something that was mine." He looked back at the flowers in blue and pink. They had been cut to showcase his mother's embroidery. "I am her child and always will be, but I am my own man too."

Once he'd said it, the words sounded trite, but Miss Quincy only nodded solemnly.

"So this is more for you and about you than anyone. That's good to know. I had put quite a bit of you into the design anyway."

"Yes." Some of the tight unhappiness left him. "The silver-smith design."

"Indeed." She secured her needle to the cloth again. "Now shall we eat? I am sure the girls have had enough time to set out a cold meal and gossip among themselves about my gentleman caller." The lightness of her tone made it into a joke between the two of them.

His smile widened at that. *Gentleman caller.* She'd said it so easily, without hesitation or regret. He stood from the bench and held out his hand to her.

Her fingers brushed his, and he realized very suddenly that her hands were bare.

Of course, they were; she was dressed for work in her own home, not going out. His hands were bare too, his gloves left with his hat at the door.

They'd never touched like this before, skin against skin.

Her hand was cool and soft except for the calluses on her fingers from so many hours spent working with a needle.

He watched her eyes widen as their hands slipped together, his fingers closing around hers, holding her but not too tightly. He could hear her take a breath in the quiet of the room. Her fingers curled slightly against his, brushing against the side of his hand, the soft, delicate space between his thumb and palm.

She took a step closer to him, even as her gaze didn't leave his.

He hadn't spent much time thinking about what it would be like to touch her and hold her, to let his hand slide around the curve of her waist, rest at the small of her back.

He thought about it now, though, with her hand in his and her looking at him with such undisguised intensity, even desire.

He was almost certain he'd never been desired before.

He reached out, bringing his other hand up. Slowly, he brushed it against her cheek. He let his hand rest there, his thumb rubbing across her soft skin. He could feel strands of her silken hair against his fingertips.

It occurred to him that he'd never seen her with her hair down, and he wondered what it would be like to push his hands into it. With the sun falling on it through the high windows, he could see the burning red among the dark strands. He wanted to trace those colors, to know what her hair smelled like if he held her close.

"Mr. Lewis," she said, her voice soft and breathless.

He drew in a breath of his own to reply, when there was the clatter of steps in the hall outside the door.

They jerked apart. Benjamin's heart was beating wildly in his chest and his cheeks were surely scarlet when one of Miss Quincy's apprentices pushed open the door.

"The noon meal is ready, Miss Quincy." Her curious gaze passed between the two of them.

"Yes, thank you," Miss Quincy said, her voice not quite as steady as it had been before he'd touched her.

They didn't look at each other as they left the workroom. Benjamin's heart was beating so hard he was certain the two women could hear it. He was trembling. He looked at the straight line of Miss Quincy's back and felt his chest fill with deep tenderness. He wanted to reach out and brush the small curls at the nape of her neck, to feel her warm skin again, but he didn't.

The three of them passed single file through a hall and down the narrow staircase to the kitchen, where the rest of Miss Quincy's girls were already seated around the table, food all set out.

Benjamin sat and took the cup of tea offered him, along with a plate of cold roast chicken, bread, and cheese. He could feel the girls' curious gazes on him. No doubt they had speculated among themselves about his relationship with their mistress. He felt his cheeks heat and wished they wouldn't watch him quite so closely.

The girls talked about a sister who was soon to be married and a Bible study they all attended together on Sunday evenings.

Benjamin suspected if he had not been there, the conversation would have been far more intimate and probably livelier. As it was they kept the conversation light, their voices politely low.

Benjamin watched Miss Quincy as much as he was able without being too obvious about his staring. He couldn't help it; every small thing about her seemed to capture his attention—the line of her throat, her hair just above her ear, the curve of her fingers around her knife, the shape of her lips as she sipped her tea, the low, patient rhythm of her voice. He was aware of all of it, his body alive with that awareness mixing with a good bit of nerves. Would things be different between them now? Would he ever be able to reach for her like that again, maybe kiss her . . .?

The meal seemed to stretch on for an eternity of careful politeness while Benjamin's mind tripped over itself with all his longings and fears.

Finally, they were done eating, and Miss Quincy's apprentices began clearing away the dishes while she saw him out into the hall.

At the front door, they paused, facing each other.

There was a respectable amount of distance between them. Miss Quincy had her hands folded primly in front of her.

Benjamin thought of her hand against his, the brush of her skin, the solid realness of finally, truly touching her, skin against skin. He wanted to reach out and take one of her hands all over again, to know if she would allow him to do it. Would she look at him again the way she'd looked at him before? The heat in her gaze back in the workroom had taken his breath away; now he just felt awkward and restless, too aware of the space between them.

Miss Quincy's gaze on him was cool and reserved—not unfriendly, but the way, Benjamin suspected, she would look at any other man.

He wanted her to reach out and take *his* hand, but that felt impossible now. He'd been so sure in that moment that she'd wanted it just as much as he had.

"Thank you for showing me your work," Benjamin said. "Would you like to accompany me to the park? Sunday, perhaps? After church?"

She hesitated, and his stomach sank. He wondered if he'd asked too much. They'd be seen together at the park —particularly on a Sunday.

"Or you could come dine with me and my sister's family," he hastened to offer. It would be in the privacy of their home where no one need know.

That thought didn't sit well with him somehow. He wanted to take her arm in public and have people see them. *Mr. Lewis, after years of being a bachelor, has finally found a lady to court,* he wanted people to say. *Lovely and talented Miss Quincy, the best quiltmaker in town. Doesn't she look fine on his arm? Isn't he lucky to have drawn the attention of such a woman?*

She was such a handsome woman, and so intelligent. He wanted to people to know she had chosen to at least spend a little time with him. That he would not be alone forever, but instead he could have this fine woman by his side.

But he'd promised to give her time and not rush this. If she didn't want to be seen in such a public place with him, he'd not press it.

"Dinner would be most welcome. Thank you for the invitation."

He smiled at her, even if his heart sank. "I look forward to it."

It had begun to rain when he stepped outside, a fine cold mist that made him hunch his shoulders against it. He might as well go back to his workshop; there was still time in the day to get some work done.

He looked back over his shoulder once he was a few paces down the street, wondering if she might be watching him and hoping that she was.

With the rain and the distance between them, he couldn't tell. He suspected she wasn't.

# Chapter 6

It was late. Remembrance sat in her sister's kitchen, drinking a cup of tea while Tabitha darned a sock.

Once it had become too dark to work, Remembrance had dismissed the girls for the day then come straight to Tabitha's house. It had been too long since the two of them had had a chance to sit and talk, what with her work and Tabitha helping her husband in his millinery shop most days.

Usually so smartly dressed and cleanly put together as befitted the mistress of such a high-class establishment, Tabitha was wearing one of her older dresses now, worn and patched in a few places, her hair coming out of its loose bun.

They each had a steaming mug of tea and were seated close enough to the hearth for Tabitha to work on the basket of mending by her feet.

"Mother says there's a gentleman in your life," Tabitha said, looking up from the cloth pulled tight across her wooden darning egg.

"There is." Remembrance shouldn't have been surprised Tabitha already knew. Gossip of all sorts moved fast through the family, and she'd said enough to her mother—even if skirting around the issue rather than addressing it directly—that pieces were easy enough to put together.

"Mr. Lewis owns the silversmith shop on Fulton Street. He's the master there."

Tabitha made an approving noise. "A silversmith? Well done, Remembrance."

Remembrance sighed. "It's far from done, Tabby. Don't act as if I'm married when we've barely seen each other a handful of times."

"But you like him?"

"I do." Remembrance took a sip of her tea. "He's a kind man, quiet, gentle, and very good at what he does. I enjoy spending time with him, it's just that . . ."

Tabitha was watching her carefully now.

"I loved Hope. She was my dearest, truest friend since we were girls. I don't make friends easily or hold many in my heart. I have not had many women in my life dear to me as Hope was, and I have never felt such tender affection for a man. She was so special, and she promised that I would be in her heart forever, so when she cut me off without a word, it was so difficult for me to bear. I am afraid of being hurt like that again. Afraid of giving my affections to someone for whom those are just easy words to be said but just as soon cast aside." Remembrance took a long, steadying breath. Revealing any part of herself was never easy, this part particularly so, but this was Tabitha, who had been there through it all.

"Do you have any reason to think Mr. Lewis's intentions aren't serious?" Tabitha asked, her voice calm and reasonable as ever.

Remembrance shook her head. "He seems serious enough about me, and he's a very sober man, but I . . . I'm still afraid."

Tabitha was silent for a moment, her gaze on her work. "I know how deep your feelings for Hope were, but the bond between a man and a woman is different. You can't compare them."

Remembrance snorted. "But I don't want them to be different." She held up one hand to forestall Tabitha's answer. "I understand, of course, that marriage is a different thing entirely, but—and this is hypothetical, mind you—if there were to be a marriage, I would want us not to be merely husband and wife but to share a far deeper, more precious bond, which can only be described as friendship."

Tabitha's expression had turned soft. "I want that for you too, for all my sisters. Marriage is one thing, but I hope and pray each of you will be married to one you can call your dearest friend."

"Not that I'm contemplating marriage to Mr. Lewis," Remembrance said quickly. "It's much too early for such thoughts. Also, I am not sure I am ready to pursue this at all. Is it terribly bad that I am both afraid that he won't want to commit to me and unsure if I want to commit to him?"

"I don't think any of your feelings are wrong, per se," Tabitha said. "But you have to decide if you want this. You cannot string this man along if you're not willing to give of yourself again."

"I already told him he could court me." Remembrance looked down at the mug of tea in her hands. "And I told him about Hope and why I was hesitant, but admitting to a fear is not the same as conquering it."

"You can change your mind about such things, but what you shouldn't do is continue to allow him to think you are interested if you aren't." Tabitha reached forward and patted Remembrance's knee. "If you want my advice, you've been alone far too long. If you like this Mr. Lewis and he's as good a man as you say, don't go looking for trouble. Allow yourself to take the chance that he could be the companion you're looking for." Tabitha set her now-darned sock aside and picked up another. "Have you met his family yet? Do you like them?"

"I met his sister," Remembrance said. "And asides from her and her husband and children, that is all the living relatives he has. Mrs. Fleming—she makes lace for some of the seamstresses in town. I like her very much."

Tabitha hummed approvingly. "Is he handsome? Do you like the way he looks?"

"He's handsome enough." Unbidden, she thought of his hand against hers and the way he'd touched her hair.

"Then stop worrying so," Tabitha said. "And Mother will tell you the same thing. Oh, which reminds me—there is a meeting I think you would be interested in attending. It's for seamstresses and women involved in other sewing crafts on how to address a possible strike at the textile mills. It will be Sunday evening at Mrs. Holloway's house. She said to tell you."

"Yes, I would very much be interested in attending. We all know the mills at Lowell are struggling; the textile mills everywhere are." Remembrance leaned forward with excitement, her hands clutching the mug. Then the realization dawned on her. "Oh, but I told Mr. Lewis I would have dinner with his family on Sunday evening."

"Sharing a family meal sounds serious on his part," Tabitha said. "If you're also serious about him, you should go."

"I know." Remembrance bit her lip. "But this meeting could be important. Not just a chance to talk about what we will do in case of a strike, but to have all of the seamstresses and women in the sewing trades in one room. You know I've been waiting for an opportunity to argue that we should formally organize."

Tabitha raised her eyebrows, dropping another mended sock into the basket. "Are you not that interested in Mr. Lewis after all? If you are, he should come first. Besides, the craftswomen of New York will never pursue formally organizing."

"We could." Remembrance bristled. "Male craftsmen organize. They represent their own interests, politically even. Why couldn't we?"

"Because the men won't like it, and the fine families who employ all of us won't like it either," Tabitha said. "The women won't agree. They won't jeopardize their businesses and risk angering the menfolk in the process."

"But separately we don't have the power to do things like set prices or put pressure on suppliers," Remembrance said. "My last supplier was chronically late with orders, and that's not an isolated incident. Suppliers are late if they don't feel there is any pressure being put on them, and they are particularly inclined to do so for female customers because they don't take us as seriously. But if we were organized, if we had a voice, things could be different."

"And I am still telling you that the ladies on Sunday won't agree," Tabitha said. "Take my advice—skip the meeting and have dinner with your man instead. There will no doubt be other meetings about the strikes. Nurturing a relationship with him and his family is more important than something that won't happen."

Remembrance was silent for a long moment. "Do you really think I'm not interested in him?"

"I don't know. Are you? From everything you've told me, he seems to be a good match for you."

Remembrance thought about his hands moving, light and delicate, across her quilting, the shock of it when their hands had touched, the slide of his bare fingers against hers, the way his lips had parted, and how intense his gaze had been. Awareness of his touch had moved from her fingertips through her, making her whole body respond to him. He'd looked so vulnerable in that moment, so open, and it had filled her with a bone-deep longing.

She wasn't sure what she would have done if Elizabeth had not interrupted them.

"I am serious about him," she said. "I might be afraid and hesitant because of that, but I like him, I do. I like him so much, Tabitha."

Tabitha sat back, looking pleased. "All right then. Now, tell me how your girls have been."

~*~

The sun was falling low in the sky as Remembrance made her way across the street and down the way toward the Lewis and Fleming house. Her stomach kept tying itself into anxious knots, and her fingers curled themselves into fists until she forced them open again.

On the doorstep she paused and took a deep breath, unclenching her hands once more and raising one to knock.

The door was opened by Mr. Lewis again, his eyes widening when he saw her. "Miss Quincy. I wasn't expecting you tonight. Come in."

"Thank you." She stepped into the hall and loosened the ribbons of her bonnet. "I'm sorry to intrude at this hour. I am sure you are just about to sit down to your meal as well, but I wanted to speak with you." She pulled her bonnet free and removed her gloves before pausing a moment to examine him.

He was without a coat again, his shirtsleeves rolled up, his hair tousled. She'd almost forgotten the impact of that look on him, the way it made her go breathless and soft inside.

"It's all right. Georgiana and Timothy aren't here this evening. They've gone to a dinner and lecture over at the Methodist church. But—oh!"

From the back of the house, Remembrance heard a baby crying. Mr. Lewis turned and hurried back down the hall with Remembrance following after.

In the kitchen Mrs. Fleming's young daughter, Charity, sat at the table eating her dinner while her baby brother sat in his cradle crying, his eyes screwed shut and his face red. Mr. Lewis scooped him up and rocked him against his chest, making soft crooning and shushing noises.

"There," he said. "There, there. It's all right now."

Charity scooted off her chair and bobbed a curtsy for Remembrance.

"Miss Fleming." Remembrance nodded back and tempered it with smile. "You don't need to be so formal. Go back to your dinner."

Charity nodded and climbed back onto her chair, picking her spoon back up. She kept her gaze on Remembrance, her eyes wide and curious.

"I am here to discuss dinner," Remembrance said, focusing her attention back on Mr. Lewis.

The baby in his arms had quieted, his small head resting against his shoulder.

"Dinner on Sunday," she clarified when he gave her a confused look. "There's a meeting of the craftswoman who do sewing also scheduled for the same time." She took a breath. "I would very much like to attend it. Not only are the topics being discussed relevant to my work, but I think us craftswomen need to meet more often to talk with each other and take steps to protect our interests. However . . ."

She took a step forward and then another until they were close enough that she could reach out and lay her hand against his arm. "I don't want you or your family to feel that I am trying to avoid dining with you when I am not. I do care very much about you, Mr. Lewis, so please tell me what other time we can meet and share a meal together or how else I can make it up to you."

Her hand rested against the curve of his upper arm, not where he was bare, but she could still feel the heat of him through the single layer of linen, feel the swell of muscle there.

"I, well . . ." His gaze seemed caught, and it took her a moment to realize that he was looking at her lips. She swallowed carefully, and finally, his gaze rose to meet hers.

She didn't back down or take her hand off his arm, though it felt like it was burning now. Like the shape of where he'd touched her would be there in the soft creases of her hand forever.

There were children in the room; she was very aware of Charity at the table still watching them and the baby in Mr. Lewis's arms.

She couldn't seem to make herself step back or look away from him, though. His gaze was like a weight against her, and the worst part was that she wanted to step into it, wanted to feel it fully on her.

He took a breath, and her gaze flicked down to his lips this time, thin but soft and pink and parted ever so slightly. His throat moved, and her gaze traced that too, the fragile flutter just under the skin as he swallowed. She wondered what it would be like to put her fingers there, to feel that motion as well as see it.

"Miss Quincy." His soft voice shocked her out of her thoughts. "If you cannot attend dinner with us on Sunday, would you consider accompanying me to the park earlier that day, around the noon hour, perhaps?"

She focused back on him. His expression seemed hesitant, with a small line of worry forming between his eyes.

"The park?" It seemed like a simple enough request until she stopped to consider it. The park would be crowded on Sunday, particularly after church. It was where people went to mingle and be social, to be *seen*. For a man and a woman to be seen together, there would be as a good as a public declaration of courting.

Mr. Lewis's gaze was still on her, still anxiously waiting. "If you don't want to . . ." He started, his voice still low but understanding.

She took a breath and thought about what Tabitha had said. "I do." She made herself smile at him. "I would love to accompany you to the park, Mr. Lewis."

"Good." He smiled back, his relief so evident it hurt her to see. A guilty sort of pain formed in her heart. "And don't worry about dinner. There will be other times, I'm sure."

"I'm sure there will." Remembrance dropped her gaze to the baby in Mr. Lewis's arms. His eyes were closed now, his fist stuffed in his mouth.

It was just a walk, she reminded herself. It wasn't as if she didn't want to be seen in public with him. She was not ashamed of this. Hesitant, yes, because already the thought of him walking away from her, of him perhaps asking another woman to the park on a Sunday, was unbearable. She could not let hesitancy rule her.

Her gaze rose again to meet his, and she let herself linger on the line of his mouth again, the kindness in his eyes. "I look forward to Sunday," she said, and this time she meant it.

# Chapter 7

They were going out to the park today. They would be seen together, him and Miss Quincy. Certainly by most of the people in his church but also a good number of other craftsmen and their families, and many of Benjamin's customers as well.

He always wore his best to church, but this morning he washed and dressed particularly carefully, his whole body thrumming with excitement.

He wondered what dress and bonnet Miss Quincy would wear and what they would talk about. Would her friends and acquaintances be there as well? Maybe her sisters, even? That thought caused a bit of anxiety to creep in, mixing with the excitement in his stomach.

He didn't taste the tea or cold leftovers they ate before they started out. He could barely hear the minister's sermon to the point where Georgiana had to nudge him several times so he could remember to recite a prayer or stand for a hymn. There was some mingling after church, of course. Georgiana stopped to speak and laugh with some of her friends while Benjamin waited patiently.

"You've been very quiet," Georgiana said as they started home.

"I'm going to meet Miss Quincy after this," Benjamin said. Charity's pace had begun to lag, so he picked her up, holding her securely on one hip as they walked. "We'll be going to the park together since she will not be able to join us for the evening meal."

Georgiana's eyebrows rose. "Well, good. If you're serious about each other, it's good that people will be able to see that." She was quiet for a moment. "But don't give too much weight to it either. If this between you and Miss Quincy doesn't last, then it doesn't."

"Why would you say that?" He looked over at her sharply.

Georgiana sighed. "I hope it does, I do with all my heart. But she's the first woman you've ever courted, the first person you've ever shown an interest in. I just don't want you to feel..." She stopped right there on the street and turned to him, reaching up to cup his cheek. "If this isn't forever, Ben, it's nothing wrong with you. Remember that."

He swallowed hard and nodded. "I will."

Benjamin helped Timothy and Georgiana get the children home, fed, and put down for their naps before checking his coat and neckcloth one more time.

"You look fine," Georgiana told him with a small fond smile as he fussed.

He bent and kissed her on the cheek. "I have to go."

Then he was off, stepping back out onto the street and heading toward Miss Quincy's house.

It was a beautiful day, the perfect day for a walk. The sky was clear and blue, and the sun was out. The air was pleasantly warm. Benjamin could feel a cold breeze coming off the water as well. It would mean that they could take their time and enjoy the weather without getting hot and uncomfortable, even with the hats and layers of clothing they'd be wearing.

When he came into view of her house, he saw Miss Quincy waiting for him on her stoop. She wore the red dress with the belt she'd worn when he'd first visited and a straw bonnet with a matching red ribbon.

"Mr. Lewis." She smiled when she saw him and came down the steps to take his arm.

"Miss Quincy. You look lovely," he said with a thrill that he could say that to her.

He was very aware of her closeness as she fell into step beside of him, aware too of the press of her gloved hand on the crook of his arm.

It was several blocks' walk to the small city park flanked by the Methodist church on one side and the Presbyterian church on the other. It was not as grand as the parks in some of the other wards; people still brought their horses to graze there, particularly on Sundays, but it was good enough for the neighborhood.

Today was beautiful and the day of rest, so there were plenty of people there as Benjamin had known there would be. There were small parties of people sitting under trees, picnicking or watching the horses. Even more people circled the park on the small footpath that looped around the edge of the grassy green. Women and men walked arm in arm with giggling children running ahead, and small groups of young women walked together. Most had just come from church and were still dressed in their Sunday finest, giving themselves an opportunity to show off a new bonnet or coat or just to enjoy the good weather and chat with friends.

They passed under the wrought-iron arch into the park and fell into step with the flow of people on the footpath.

Benjamin tried to keep his gaze on the path ahead of them, mostly so he didn't run into anyone on the crowded walkway.

Little things about Miss Quincy keep distracting his attention, though—the soft skin of her throat just above the collar of her dress or the dark wisps of hair at the nape of her neck that her bonnet didn't quite cover.

He cleared his throat. "So have you been to any more botany lectures?" he asked, wanting to start the conversation off as lightly as he could.

Miss Quincy pushed her glasses back up her delicate nose and tipped her head to look at him around the brim of her bonnet. "Unfortunately not. The Friends of the Botanical Club have not been invited to take part in another open lecture, but I suspect there will be more, perhaps further into the semester. And what about you, Mr. Lewis? Have you read any more poetry?"

It took him a moment to recall their conversation about Mr. Bryant and his work. He shook his head. "Like you, I haven't had the pleasure of another public reading."

They fell into silence for a moment, their pace slow as they circled the park.

There were trees along the path, not enough to say that it was lined by trees but enough to shade their way. Benjamin wondered what sort they were. They were not oak or maple; those he could identify. Miss Quincy would surely know. He was about to ask when they came abreast of an older couple Benjamin recognized from church.

He nodded to them. The elderly man smiled pleasantly enough as he always did, while his wife pretended not to notice Benjamin's presence at all as she always did.

Miss Quincy frowned as they passed the couple. Benjamin's stomach lurched, wondering if she would ask or comment. She didn't and they walked on, leaving the couple behind.

Up ahead a small knot of people had formed, interrupting the stream. As they drew closer, Benjamin saw it was three or four older men with newspapers tucked under their arms.

"My entire career I've designed whaling ships, and I am telling you Arctic exploration is impossible," one said quite heatedly, his round face and balding head pink from passion and possibly also the sun.

"But with coal engines—" started one of his companions, a gray-haired man with spectacles and a coat badly in need of patching.

"A fool's errand!" the pink-faced man cut him off. "From an engineering perspective, it cannot be done. I don't care how brave or foolhardy your crew is, the ships themselves won't survive such a crossing."

"But—" another member of the group began.

Benjamin and Miss Quincy passed them by and left them arguing about it. When Benjamin looked back over at Miss Quincy, she was smiling, and it made him smile too. He wondered if he should perhaps inquire about the trees.

Her smile slid away as they turned the corner. "That couple we passed," she said, and Benjamin knew he wasn't going to be able to avoid that conversation. "Did they know you?"

"They attend our church."

She took that in for a moment. "Does she always ignore you?"

Benjamin sighed. "Yes. Some people do."

She threw him a sharp glance sparkling with anger, although he thought it was not at him. "*Really?* How extremely rude! I can't imagine."

He fidgeted. He couldn't help it; he hated talking about this. They were coming to a clear spot on the path without many people around them, so he paused and took her hands in his. "I wasn't raised like this, you know. Not as a man—well, a boy. My mother raised me to be a girl, and this"—he let go of one of her hands to gesture at his own body—"was a choice I made."

She looked at him, her gaze very serious behind her glasses. "I know."

He let his breath out in a small sigh, somewhere between hurt and disappointment. "Oh."

"Not that there's anything wrong with the way you are or the kind of man you are," she hurried to add. "It's just that the first time we met, I could tell that was who you used to be but also not who you were anymore, which is why I've never brought it up." She looked down at the path between their feet and then back up at him. "Did I say the wrong thing?"

"No." It was a small blow to his ego easily washed away by his relief at the fact that she'd known and agreed to be courted by him anyway.

"Do people treat you like that often?" she asked, her features pinching into a frown all over again.

"Not everyone is so hostile, obviously. I run a good business, I attend the local church, and I have friends. Most people accept me at face value as they should. It's really all I want, but I discomfort some people simply by existing. Often they don't even realize why they feel uncomfortable, they just do, and they tend to take it out on me."

Miss Quincy drew in an angry breath through her nose.

"Does it bother you? That some people might treat me like that?" He hesitated for a moment, then added, "And by extension, you?"

"Of course it bothers me," she snapped, and Benjamin's heart sank even lower.

His fingers tightened around hers. "I understand. If you were with many other men, no one would look twice at you."

"I'm not worried about me," Miss Quincy said with passion, seeming to bristle all over. "I'm worried about you. You're a good man; how could they treat you so poorly? If she does it again next time we meet, I'll give her a piece of my mind."

"Ah, well," Benjamin said, slightly worried about the possibility of Miss Quincy accosting an elderly church lady in the name of defending his honor. "I'm sure that won't be necessary. She's very old. Just smile and move on. That's what I try to do."

"No one is too old to learn to treat people kindly and with respect."

Someone behind them coughed, and they turned to see a middle-aged lady waiting for them to stop blocking the path. Miss Quincy took his arm again and they continued on.

a short ways from them was a small tree under which no one was sitting, and Miss Quincy guided Benjamin over to it so they could speak in relative privacy without blocking the walkers on the path.

Miss Quincy settled herself on the grass under the tree, her skirts folded neatly around her. "May I tell you something?"

"Certainly." He couldn't think of what else to do, so he settled beside her.

"I told you that I'd been courted before."

"Yes." By someone who had broken her heart. Benjamin remembered the look of tightly controlled hurt on her face when she'd told him.

"Her name was Hope," she said. "She was my best friend, and I loved her very much." She looked down at her hands against the cloth of her skirt. "For a long time, I thought I'd never be able to call someone else 'friend' again, the way I called her that. But I want to with you. So." She straightened her back and looked at him. "Now you've told me one of yours, and I've told you mine. A secret for a secret." She held her hand out, palm up in the grass between them.

Not reaching for his but letting him come to her.

"Thank you." He placed his hand in hers, letting his fingers slide into the spaces between hers.

# Chapter 8

Mr. Lewis escorted her to Mrs. Holloway's house.

"You don't have to wait." Remembrance told him at the steps leading to the front door.

"Nonsense. It will be an hour? Maybe a bit longer? I'll buy a paper to read and then escort you home."

She wanted to argue, but she didn't much feel like walking home alone in the failing light either. She nodded. "An hour, no longer. I promise."

She climbed the steps and knocked on the door. A girl in a pretty apron opened the door.

"Miss Quincy, quiltmaker," Remembrance introduced herself.

The girl nodded. "This way, Miss. Mother's expecting you."

She led Remembrance to a small parlor already packed with women. Women of all ages sat on every chair and clustered around a small table with tea laid out. They also stood against the walls or together in small groups, wherever there was room. Remembrance squeezed herself between Mrs. Miller, a seamstress she'd met a time or two before, and a young woman she didn't know in a dark blue dress. The woman nodded and smiled at Remembrance.

"All right ladies," Mrs. Holloway said in a voice that carried. "As you know, we are gathered here today to discuss the unfortunate state of cloth manufacture and trade."

An unhappy murmur went up around the room.

"Well, at least with so many new mills opening up, we aren't suffering from want of choice," one older woman with a round face and graying hair said optimistically.

"If you like cheap cloth your lady clients are sure to complain about," the woman sitting next to her put in darkly. "No mill-made cloth will ever be as fine as hand woven."

"But no lady is willing to pay for a dress made of hand-woven cloth," another woman put in, shaking her head. "We aren't here to debate the merits or craftsmanship of mill-made cloth. The moment for that has long passed."

"Competition among the mill owners means prices have dropped," Mrs. Holloway said. "Particularly for those of us who sew with cotton cloth, but linen has dropped as well. That might be good for us over the short term, but it also means that mill owners have been lowering wages in an attempt to make up the difference, and that *will* lead to a strike among the girls. The question before us now is how we will handle it."

"Not much we can do," said Mrs. Green, one of the oldest and most accomplished seamstresses Remembrance personally knew. "Cloth shortages happen. The ladies will have to live with that, and we will all have to learn to live with hard times. I remember before the mills when we relied primarily on cloth from England. Not a pretty picture, particularly with the tariffs on imported cloth being what they are. Even if there is a strike, things will never be that hard, not now with so many domestic mills springing up."

"Or we could support the mill girls," Remembrance said.

There was a rustle as all the ladies in the room turned to look at her. She saw recognition on more than a few faces along with a certain amount of displeasure. She was known to some of the women there for her support of the ban on slave-grown cotton and not well loved among the ones who made their living off sewing the increasingly fashionable cotton dresses.

She fought not to shift under the heavy weight of their combined gazes. Sweat began to prick along the back of her neck, both from the sudden scrutiny and the heat of the overfull room. "If we support the strike or put pressure on the mill owners not to lower wages, we have a better chance of having the labor dispute solved before cloth becomes short," Remembrance pushed on. "We also make ourselves friends of the mill girls. They are women who work in textiles too. "

"Hardly the same," one of the seamstresses said in a prim, disdainful tone into the stifling silence. "We are highly skilled ladies of the higher feminine crafts, while mill girls are increasingly uneducated immigrant women."

"Not to mention, Miss Quincy, that some of our clients are daughters or wives of mill owners or their equals in society. Can any of us afford to go against them?" Mrs. Green asked, regarding Remembrance closely over the top of her spectacles. "Mark my words, there is no man who has made his fortune in industry who will look kindly on a craftsman or woman who supports the unionization of workers."

There was a contemplative silence.

Remembrance pressed her lips tightly together and clasped her hands in front of her, trying not to bump with the women pressed in on either side.

Supporting a strike would be the right thing to do, but Mrs. Green was also correct that Remembrance's trade lived and died by the good opinion of the ladies and, by extension, their husbands. To throw that away after she had sacrificed so much would be unthinkable.

*Pick your battles,* she reminded herself. At least they were meeting, all the craftswoman together in one room to discuss these sorts of things.

"We should form a society."

Remembrance snapped around to look at the woman who'd said what she'd been thinking, narrowly avoiding ramming her shoulder into the young woman who stood beside her.

Lydia Hawthorn sat with a cup of tea in one gloved hand, fanning herself gently with the other, looking every inch the fashionable young lady. She specialized in embroidery and finishing work on dresses and had become quite well known for her abilities to take an older dress and make it fashionable again. It was quite a popular and lucrative skill, even among the upper classes.

"Like a church society," Lydia said, smiling at all the ladies around her. "Or a benevolent association, but for us ladies involved in the finer feminine crafts. Some way for us to come together like we are today and make these sorts of decisions. Maybe even appeal to the better nature of some gentleman merchants."

"I don't think it's our place—" someone started from the other end of the room.

"She's right," the girl standing next to Remembrance put in. "I have such a dreadful time with my thread merchant overselling me, but if I and some of the other seamstresses were to speak with him as a group—"

There was a babble of voices.

"Enough!" Mrs. Holloway bellowed, cutting through the noise and causing most of the women to fall silent. "We will set aside the question of a formal society for another time. Although Miss Hawthorn does make a good point. For now, we will agree that in the case of a strike among the mill girls, we will each handle our own clients accordingly."

Which felt like another way of saying they had done all this talking for nothing. Remembrance bit her tongue and reminded herself that it was good they'd come together at all and that Lydia's proposal had not been dismissed out of hand.

The meeting broke up.

Some of the women stayed to talk among themselves, sharing the latest news and catching up, but most headed for the door.

Remembrance caught up with Lydia in the hall.

"Thank you for the suggestion of a society," she said. "I do agree with you. It would be wise for us to organize."

Lydia smiled at Remembrance as they both stepped out of Mrs. Holloway's house and back onto the street. "Well, thank you, Miss Quincy, for suggesting we support those poor mill girls, although I knew it was far too radical a notion for most of the others to agree to. But still, you tried."

"Miss Hawthorn, Miss Quincy." Mrs. Green descended the stairs. Her impeccable white coif was now hidden under a slightly faded black satin bonnet. "There has never been a society of seamstresses, quiltmakers, and finishing women." She fixed them both with a stern look. "However, it may be time for that to change. It is very easy for women in a trade to be taken advantage of and very difficult for us to make changes for our own benefit, but perhaps we stand more of a chance acting together."

A cart pulled up in front of them, and a young man jumped down from the seat. "Grandmother." He took Mrs. Green's hand.

She gave Lydia and Remembrance one more considering look, then let him help her up onto the seat of the cart.

That suddenly reminded Remembrance of Mr. Lewis. She looked around, wondering if he'd gone off somewhere or maybe hadn't waited for her after all.

But no, he was waiting, leaning against the fence with a newspaper tucked under his arm.

Remembrance felt her chest fill with relief at the sight of him, familiar and solid.

"Is that your gentleman?" Lydia asked.

"I—" Remembrance took a very deep breath. "Yes, he is, and I should go meet him. I hope we can talk later."

"I hope so too," Lydia said and sounded like she meant it. She gave Remembrance one last bright smile and headed off in the opposite direction.

By herself now, Remembrance crossed the distance to where Mr. Lewis stood.

"How was the meeting?" he asked, offering her his arm. "Did it go well?"

"It went very well," she said. "Very well, indeed. I think we are going to do it. Tabitha said they wouldn't, but I think it might actually happen."

Mr. Lewis blinked. "What will happen?"

Remembrance took a breath. "The needlework women of New York are going to start a professional society. My older sister, Mrs. Wells, said the ladies would never agree, but Miss Hawthorn suggested it this evening, and I do believe we will form it."

"That's good." Mr. Lewis smiled.

"We didn't come to any definitive conclusion about the possibility of strikes." Remembrance amended. "But we have time. There isn't a strike yet. One isn't even planned as far as I know, but there will almost certainly be one in the future." She sighed. "I tried to convince them to support the girls when they do strike, but I don't think they will. It would mean forming a public alliance with women a lot of the ladies here today feel are beneath them. Still, it would strengthen our position, I think, bringing our power to bear, as it were, as well as being the moral thing to do."

They headed off arm and arm, back down the street toward Remembrance's house. It was not quite dark yet. The sky was a grey-blue above them, shadowed but not yet properly night.

"Is that what you want?" Mr. Lewis asked. "A needlework women's society with power to support other working women?"

"Of course." Remembrance twisted her skirts out of the way as she walked. "I want to know I've built something important. A society that would give us some power to better our craft and our place and help other women in similar industries is exactly what I want."

"What? Is being a Friend of the Botanical Club of Columbia University not enough of a legacy?" His eyes crinkled into a gently teasing smile.

"Oh, being a Friend of the Botanical Club of Columbia University will also be my legacy. Did you know New York used to have botanical gardens before they were sold because the city couldn't maintain them? They might one day have them again. There are those in the Botanical Club who have been talking about it. If they do build the gardens again, I shall give money to help with their funding. Then there will be a small plaque somewhere in the gardens to commemorate the generosity of Miss Remembrance Quincy." Remembrance said lightly, smiling at him. "But I also want to be remembered for helping to found the first ever society of seamstresses and other craftswomen."

That way she'd be sure to leave behind a legacy whether or not her quilts were signed or bore a maker's mark.

The thought dimmed her joy.

"And there will be your work," Mr. Lewis said quietly from beside her as he if was aware of her unhappy thoughts. "Your quilts will be your legacy too."

She could tell he truly believed it, and it made some of the unhappiness in her chest loosen.

Her quilts would still exist even without a maker's mark. They would still be admired, valued, and even envied. Her skills would be passed down, living on through the girls she trained and the girls they would train in turn.

The passing of her craft from her hands to the hands of the other women who would hold a needle after her would be her true legacy. The thought of that was a comfort in a way, as was having him acknowledge it.

"You're right," she said. "I hope to be known for many things in my life. What about you, Mr. Lewis? What will you be remembered for?"

For a long moment, he didn't say anything to that.

She glanced sideways at him as they walked, watching his brow furrow ever so slightly as if he was deep in thought before he answered.

"I don't know if I hope to be remembered for much. That I had a family who loved me and that I loved in returned and supported well, I suppose. But besides that." He paused again and seemed to mull it over further. "If any of the things I have made were to last," he said finally. "I would like that one day, someone might think that I made a very enjoyable teapot."

She couldn't help it. She laughed. "An enjoyable teapot?"

His lips turned up too, his smile echoing hers. "Well, yes. Teapots are made to be enjoyed. Silver teapots, in particular, are made to be beautiful, to brighten a dull morning or add a bit of elegance to a tea set. Most importantly, they are made to hold tea, and no one makes tea who doesn't enjoy it."

Remembrance tilted her head. "I suppose you're right."

"Although if someone were to say I made a fine spoon, I'd be just as pleased," Mr. Lewis said. "The things that I make might be made of silver, but many of them are supposed to be ordinary household things. So if, in the future, they are still bringing people ordinary household pleasure, then I'll be well content."

He sounded like he meant it too.

She looked at him, wondering if he could really be fulfilled by such small victories, but he seemed sincere and satisfied in his answer.

He reached over with his free hand to cover hers where it was still pressed into the crook of his arm, drawing her back out of her thoughts.

"We are almost there. It has been a very lovely day, Miss Quincy. Thank you for sharing it with me."

Her mouth curved up in a small smile. "Even the part where you waited on the street for over an hour for me?"

He smiled back. "I will wait outside of many meetings if you want me to." His fingers squeezed hers. "This was important to you tonight. I want to value the things that are important to you, even if I don't share in them. That is part of what friendship is, to my way of thinking at least."

They'd come to her house and both stopped in front of the gate. He turned toward her, studying her face in the dim evening light. "I would like to be your friend."

For a moment she froze. *My dearest friend.* She took a breath. "I would like that too, Mr. Lewis."

On impulse, she leaned toward him, close enough that she could feel his breath ghost across her cheek. This close, he smelled like clean linen, a little like sweat from their walk, and sage and rosemary from his soap.

She kissed him gently on the cheek. Her lips just brushed his skin, but still, she felt it, right down to the ache that bloomed in the center of her chest with nervousness and longing.

They were so close she could hear his breath catch. He drew it in on a small sound as if to say something.

But she turned before he could and pushed the gate open, heading up the steps to the house.

# Chapter 9

The teapot sat on the worktable in front of him. Benjamin gazed down at it with a certain amount of displeasure. It was mocking him, he was sure of it. He'd spent the morning doing small repair jobs, jewelry and men's buckles that really only needed soldering to make whole again. He'd even made a few spoons instead of leaving that sort of busywork for the apprentices, trying to put off this moment as long as he could.

The general shape of the teapot was there—an inverted pear-shaped body, pleasingly round at the top and tapering down at the base, with an elegant curving S-shaped spout. It was just . . . very plain. When he'd first started, he'd imagined it delicate and pristine in its simplicity, but now, sitting on his worktable, it just looked commonplace and uninteresting. He should have gone with a scalloped body instead.

There was still the engraving to do once the actual shape of the piece was completed. Benjamin still had the design she'd drawn laid out on his worktable. It would add something, that lovely leaf design, but he was afraid that it would still be too plain.

He picked it up and dusted some of the metal shavings off it, holding it between his hands. He'd seen her work, the image of white linen and entwining vines, leaves, and flowers had been foremost in his mind the entire time he'd been working on this piece. He wanted this teapot to prove to her that he was just as talented in his own medium as she was. He wanted her to be able to see the fine precision of her own work mirrored here. When she saw this piece for the first time, as incomplete as it might be, he wanted her to be filled with the same sense of wonder that he had been when he'd sat next to her in her quilting workroom.

Most of all, he wanted her to like it.

He was terribly afraid she wouldn't. She'd look at the teapot and see it as plain, ugly, and imperfect. Looking at it now, he could see every flaw writ large, every place where his hammer had slipped, where the mold hadn't been carved quite as smoothly as it should have, or where he hadn't wielded his file with quite enough care or skill.

He sighed and put the teapot down.

Miss Quincy was coming that evening to look at it. Georgiana had been excited about her visit all day. They were going to talk, and Georgiana was, in her own words, going to find out everything about Miss Quincy. Benjamin, on the other hand, had spent the entire day in a state of increasing anxiety. He'd gone to the shop early, before the sun was even up, for just that reason, catching up on chores that no one usually had the time to get to before throwing himself into his work.

His mind kept jumping to her pleased smile as they had teased each other on the way home the night before, the memory of the weight of her hand on his arm, the press of her soft lips against his cheek.

His stomach knotted, tight and painful. He was sure she wasn't going to like the teapot.

Behind him, Timothy and the boys clattered around the shop. Benjamin tried to focus on the silverwork in his hands and think about it from a purely artistic perspective, putting aside his anxiousness for a moment.

A scrollwork handle would fit well with the overall design. It would mirror the spout without being too obvious and add some extra detail to the overall simplicity of the piece. Something to draw the eye while complementing the unadorned curve of the body of the pot.

He put the pot aside and reached for his sketch pad. They already had a mold for the shape he wanted to cast; he'd work the shape afterward while the metal was still hot, making it just the way he wanted. He needed to know the exact shape that would suit best, though, and that meant drawing it out.

Mr. Samuel, the silversmith to whom Benjamin had originally been apprenticed, had never drawn out any designs. He didn't need to, he'd told Benjamin once; the shape of what he wanted to make lived inside his mind and his hands. There was no need to waste expensive paper.

Benjamin envied that skill; it was one he'd never learned. Small, easy pieces he could do without drawing. Spoons or buckles he could make in his sleep. Larger pieces, though, needed to be sketched out down to the last detail before he could make them.

He wondered if Miss Quincy was the same way.

His stomach twisted up again at the thought of her, his nerves spiking.

With some effort, he forced his thoughts back to the design he still needed to finalize. Pulling over a stool, he reached for his sketch pad and tried not to think about Miss Quincy at all.

~*~

The knock at the door came after the children had been put to bed for the night. Aveline had gone to her room, so Benjamin went to answer it.

"Good evening, Mr. Lewis." Miss Quincy smiled at him from where she stood on the front step.

"Good evening."

He still felt jittery. His stomach had been clenching and unclenching for most of the day, but he didn't feel quite so anxious now. Having Miss Quincy actually there helped. It was so much easier to get wrapped up in thoughts of failure, disappointing her, or embarrassing himself when he couldn't see her smile.

He stepped back from the door. "Please come in."

She entered the hall, undid the ribbons of her bonnet, hung the bonnet on one of the hat-pegs, and then turned back to him. "Lead the way, Mr. Lewis."

Georgiana and Timothy were still sitting at the table in the kitchen when Benjamin came back, Miss Quincy following along behind him.

They both rose when they saw her. Timothy gave her a nod and a smile, and Georgiana came forward, her hands extended.

"Miss Quincy, so good to see you again. Please come in, sit. I have some cider heating."

"Thank you." Miss Quincy smiled, and Georgiana clasped her hands briefly before moving on to the hearth and the pot of cider hanging over the flames.

Benjamin pulled one of the worn wooden chairs out. Miss Quincy sat and folded her small strong hands on the tabletop in front of her. Benjamin's gaze was caught by those hands, the smallness of them belying their skill.

She was wearing the dark gold dress again, the one with the vibrant flowery print and a few carefully mended holes. This also put his mind at ease. It was so obviously a working dress, not something to be seen in, because she had come here after a long day's work to rest and drink hot cider by the fire.

He took a calming breath and sat beside her at the table.

Georgiana poured them all cups of cider. Benjamin wrapped his fingers around the warm mug and inhaled some of the sweet, tart steam. Benjamin had never been much for cider poured from a pitcher that had been left to sit on the table until it had gone tepid. He liked a cup of hot cider in the evenings, though, when the wind off the ocean was cold and he and his family were tucked up safe inside their house.

Miss Quincy picked up her own mug and sipped her cider carefully, the steam curling around her face as she did.

"Benjamin tells me you have a passion for botany," Georgiana said, seating herself beside Timothy.

"Yes. I've always been interested in the science of it and the mystery of it, I suppose—the way plants grow, the shape of their leaves and flowers, how different they are from each other, even the ones we know to be very closely related. There's such beauty in variety like that. But also botany was an interest my parents approved of. I don't think they would have been so terribly pleased if I had loved mathematics or chemistry." Her lips turned up in a small smile as if this was a joke, and Georgiana smiled back, just as amused.

"Perhaps not. Although it is good and necessary to travel one's own path sometimes, even if others, particularly parents, don't approve," Georgiana said, and for the briefest of moments, Benjamin felt her gaze rest on him, intense enough to make his skin prickle with it.

Miss Quincy took another sip of her cider. "I agree with you, although I tend to choose my battles. I have no problem with studying botany or working at a craft my parents approve of. When I do choose to travel my own path despite what people might think, it tends to be over other issues—abolition and a woman's right to conduct her business fairly. Other times, it's when people's liberty and right to live a safe and dignified life is on the line. That I would never knowingly do anything to endanger."

Unlike Georgiana, Miss Quincy's gaze never wavered, and she did not so much as glance in his direction.

Still, Benjamin couldn't help but hunch his shoulders over his cider, his cheeks and the tips of his ears heating.

Georgiana smiled, looking satisfied.

Timothy cleared his throat. "Yes, well, perhaps it would be a good idea for Benjamin to show you the progress we've made on your commission."

Benjamin put his cup down and pushed himself back from the table harder than he'd meant to. His chair scraped loudly across the floor, making them all turn to look at him as he got to his feet. He was keenly aware of their eyes as he left the room and came back with the teapot wrapped in a soft cloth.

He set it on the table and unwrapped it. He'd polished it, even though polishing was generally a waste before the piece was complete. Benjamin did try to clean pieces before clients saw them, and he'd wanted it to look its best when Miss Quincy saw this particular piece.

He carefully lifted it off the cloth and put it on the table before sitting back down in his chair. The handle wasn't affixed yet; he'd cast it already, but the filing and making sure the details were as he wanted them would take time still. The shape was there, though, and he hoped it would give her a good sense of what the pot would look like in the end.

There was a moment of silence as they all looked at it. Benjamin dropped his hands into his lap, his fingers twisting together.

He'd put Miss Quincy in a bad position, he thought belatedly, showing her the piece in front of his family. She could do nothing but praise it regardless of how she actually felt. His gaze went to her face, watching carefully for any sign of politely concealed displeasure. He should trust that she was professional enough that if she did want something changed, she'd find a way to say it, but he was too much a jumble of nerves right now to let that thought soothe him at all.

Miss Quincy drew in a long breath. "It's lovely." She met his gaze and beamed.

He'd seen her smile plenty of times over their acquaintance, but those had mostly been small smiles of amusement or affection. So many of her emotions were controlled and focused down into an intensity he admired very much, but the way she was looking at him right now was pure uncomplicated happiness.

His hands unknotted below the table and he leaned forward. "You think so?"

Her gaze moved from his face to the silver. "I love the shape." She reached forward, the palm of her hand carefully skimming down the inverted pear shape of the body. "Almost tall and long the way silver teapots used to be but with a round fullness too. I've never seen one shaped like this—bigger at the top than the bottom."

"It's not very common," Benjamin agreed. "Although it's hardly an original design. I saw one like this once in a shop selling imports from the Netherlands, I think, and I always had the shape in my mind as something I'd like to make." His hand joined hers, tracing the side of the pot. "I tried to make the length of the handle and spout balance it. Do you not think it's too plain? I know there's the engraving still to do around the top." He marked the place with his fingertips.

"Not at all," Miss Quincy said. "It's made of silver." Her finger traced the swooping curve of the spout. "This will be a beautiful piece as it is with only a small amount of engraving added. A spout shaped like a peacock is all well and good for some, but it doesn't suit me at all."

Finally, Benjamin's chest loosened and he could breathe normally again. "No. I suppose it doesn't."

"But this teapot will suit me very well," Miss Quincy said, looking so pleased.

Benjamin felt his own heart lift in response.

Georgiana cleared her throat, and for the first time in several minutes, Benjamin remembered that they weren't alone at the table.

That fact seemed to catch Miss Quincy off guard too, and she focused back on Georgiana and Timothy, both of whom were smiling.

"I still have some work to do on it," Benjamin said, reaching for the pot to wrap it back up again. "So if you want me to change something or add something else, just let me know. I was also thinking of doing a small creamer or a sugar bowl as well if you'd like."

"I don't use sugar," Miss Quincy said, which reminded him that he had never seen a sugar bowl in her coffee service. "A creamer would be lovely, though. If you think it won't be too much, that is."

He snorted. "You're making me an entire quilt. I can make you a creamer."

"As long as you think it's an equitable exchange."

"It would be." He knew some of the amount of time that went into making a quilt, and besides, he wanted to do this for her.

He finished wrapping the teapot while the conversation turned to other things. Georgiana asked after Miss Quincy's sisters and mother, wanting to know all the details about their husbands and children, what they did for a living, and what church they went to.

Miss Quincy told her, her soft voice washing over Benjamin like water. He didn't really listen as much as he allowed himself to slowly unwind. The nervousness he'd carried inside him finally untangled itself, leaving him feeling calm and strangely weightless. He found his gaze going back to her over and over again, mapping the shape of her face, her hands, the soft curve of her mouth.

She looked so right there in his kitchen, sipping cider and filling Georgiana in on all the details of her nieces and nephews' lives.

He wanted to kiss her.

He wanted to take her in his arms right there in the kitchen and feel the way her body would curve against his, fitting them together like the answer to a question he'd been asking himself for a long time now. She would be warm in his arms, and her lips would be soft and taste like sweet, tart apples. He imagined her smile against his mouth, imagined the silken feel of her hair against his hands. He imagined her kissing him back.

Even with Georgiana and Timothy sitting there too, kissing her would be right and natural and so very good.

He wanted to do more than just imagine it.

He didn't move, though.

Instead, he sat and watched her talk and drank his cider.

For all his fantasies, now was not the time. He'd promised not to push her, and he'd already pushed her far more than he should have. They needed to speak and make sure that she was as ready as he was.

Also, he wanted the first time he kissed her to be private, a moment of intimacy shared between just the two of them.

Soon, though. He wanted it to be soon. Every part of his body sang with that, making his skin prickle with anticipation for it.

When their cups were empty and the conversation had come to its natural conclusion, Miss Quincy rose.

"Thank you for your hospitality," she said to Georgiana and Timothy. "But I should get home to bed."

"Of course. Thank you so much for coming, and I hope you come again soon." Georgiana rose as well and came around the table to clasp Miss Quincy's hands one last time.

Benjamin followed Miss Quincy back into the front hall and watched her put her bonnet back on.

"May I walk you home?" he asked, and she turned to look at him. "It's just that it's terribly dark out. I don't want you to have to do it alone."

Miss Quincy hesitated for a moment but nodded. "I would like that."

He nodded and took her arm.

Outside, the sky was dark, clouds covering most of the stars and shrouding the streets in deep shadow.

Luckily the city rarely slept, and light spilled out of nearly every house and building. Carriages and omnibuses hung with lanterns clattered by on the streets, and people passed back and forth with lanterns of their own.

Still, the streets and particularly the alleyways were dark enough to keep Benjamin alert and watchful as they traversed the few blocks between his house and hers.

"Your family seems very lovely," Miss Quincy said as they walked. She was silent for a moment, then she asked, "Did Mr. Fleming make your sister the silver tea service she used the first time I came to call?"

"Yes," Benjamin said distractedly. "He gave it to her as a gift when they were wed, to start their new household with."

Miss Quincy didn't say anything to that, just walked on beside him.

"He's a very fine silversmith," Benjamin offered.

"I'm sure he is." She looked up at him, and he thought she was about to say something else, but she shook her head instead.

They came to a stop in front of the gate to her house, and she let go of his arm.

"Thank you, Mr. Lewis. I had a lovely evening."

"So did I," he said breathlessly, not able to keep all of his emotions out of his voice.

She gave him a small, strangely tight smile and pushed open her front gate.

He watched her walk up the front path and disappear into the house before turning to retrace his steps back to his own house.

# Chapter 10

Remembrance sat at her quilting frame.

The sun was going down, casting the room in deep reds and dark golden yellows. Her girls moved around the room, talking softly as they put things away and swept scraps of thread and stray dust off the floor. They'd leave to go back to their own homes soon. On a normal day, she'd eat her dinner alone and heat a brick on the stove to take with her to her room for the night.

Secretly, the moment when she wrapped a hot brick in a flannel cloth and carried it carefully against her chest into her bedroom was one of her favorite parts of the day. The solid heat of the brick against her cramped and aching hands felt so good after a long day of sewing.

If her hands weren't hurting her too much, she'd write in her journal before bed, cataloging the day's work, noting any ideas she had for future projects, and sometimes putting in an extra note about the weather.

That was on a normal evening, but this evening, Mr. Lewis would call on her to see her progress on the quilt.

She drew one finger across just the edge of it. Her mind went back to when he'd first come to her and she'd thought this quilt had been meant as a wedding gift for a fiancée like so many of the quilts she'd sewn over the years.

Quilts were for weddings, for new houses, new babies, and new beginnings.

Just like the teapot Mr. Fleming had given Mrs. Fleming as a wedding gift. Like the teapot Mr. Lewis was making for her now. Would he want marriage? That was what others would expect for them, where this courting would end up. Not the friendship she craved by marriage.

Remembrance pulled back her hand and let it fall to her lap.

What were they doing?

What was *she* doing?

She had met his family, had been escorted by him in public, and was making him a quilt, for pity's sake.

People would look at them and expect things, her family and his, the sorts of things that were expected between a man and a woman, the ones she'd never wanted for herself.

She'd been told once, long ago, that men and women could not be friends the way she and Hope had been.

The pain of that, of *expectation*, was a like a cold fist closing around her heart.

And yet . . . she thought about sitting in his kitchen, walking in the park with the sun on her face, the sound of his laughter or his voice, soft and faltering as he recited poetry.

She gazed helplessly at the patterns of flowers and leaves she'd created for him.

She liked him. She really liked him.

And she didn't want to stop—didn't want to not talk to him or go on walks with him, hear him laugh, or sit by the fire with him on a cold evening.

"Friends," he'd said, and it was like he'd reached into her and found her most secret longing.

Would he be just that? Her most beloved, cherished friend?

The girls had bustled out of the room while she'd been lost in thought, so she was alone when the knock came on her sitting room door.

It startled her. She'd anticipated the bell and having to go down into the front hall herself to let Mr. Lewis in.

Instead, he was right there, standing outside her door looking apologetic.

"One of your apprentices let me in the front door on her way out," he said. "I hope that was all right. I don't want to get you in trouble with your landlady."

"It's fine." She stood back to let him in.

It was unusual, but he was a legitimate a client for whom she was doing work. As long as she wasn't making a habit of having strange men over during the evenings, her landlady wouldn't complain.

"How has your day been?" Mr. Lewis asked, stepping into the sitting room, his gentle gaze for her and her alone.

"All right." She smoothed a hand down her skirts, feeling strangely shy. "And yours?"

His eyes crinkled at the corners as he smiled. "Well enough. Do you want to show me your progress on the quilt?"

"Of course." She led the way into the workroom and over to the quilting frame.

The last of the evening sun spilled across the cloth, picking out the stitch work and the brushstrokes of delicate color where Remembrance had used pieces of the dresses he'd brought her.

His eyes widened, his breath catching. He reached forward to run his hand across the leaves and vines of the border.

He'd seen it before in a rougher stage, but now it was almost complete. Not quite a finished piece, but close. Remembrance and her girls would move on to a new large project soon, a quilted wedding dress for a paper merchant's daughter. Still, his quilt would have her full attention until it was complete.

"What do you think?" she asked, watching him trace the leaves.

"It's beautiful. You do such fine work." He sat on the bench next to the frame, his eyes still on the quilt. "I love how this looks." He touched the cloth appliquéd into flower petals and closed buds. "Not garish at all but lovely."

"Hm." She sat beside him, her gaze more critical on her work, picking out a crooked stitch here and there, and all the loose threads she was going to have to tidy up.

"She made these dresses for me," he said suddenly, his fingers still lingering on the cloth, his gaze far away. "She used to make many dresses for me, and bonnets and pretty shawls. Almost as if she thought that if she made enough of them, made them feminine enough, I'd come to want them. If she dressed me up enough, made me pretty enough, told me how beautiful I was often enough, I'd become her daughter. Like deep down that was what she thought a woman was—a pretty dress and someone to tell her that she was beautiful enough." He looked up at Remembrance, his gaze searching her face for a moment, taking her in down to the last detail. "But that's not true. That isn't what we are. There is part of my spirit that will never make me a woman, even as there is part of yours that always will be no matter what clothes you choose to wear." His eyes went back to the quilt again and he sighed. "But she still tried. Until the day she died, she still tried."

Remembrance didn't know what to say to that.

There had been moments when she'd been young, when she'd loved Hope and struggled against the world, moments when she'd wished with all her heart that she had been born different. She'd wished she and Hope could have been husband and wife.

Those were only moments, though, and she knew he was right that there was no part of her that was not a woman, complicated and difficult though that might be. She'd gloried in it, had gloried in it with Hope; the places where they were the same as well as where they were different had both been beautiful to her. It was beautiful to her now with him, if beautiful in a different way. Yet seeing that about herself allowed her to see the truth in him; as she was, he was not, like pieces carved from the same wood but made different from each other. There was a part of them what was different, beautifully and elegantly so, but it was certainly not something as simple as clothes or names or social customs.

The silence had stretched on too long.

He was watching her, waiting for her to say something, his mouth turning down ever so slightly as the moments passed, his eyes clouding in doubt.

She reached out and took his hand in hers, feeling the strength in his grip, the calluses and warm skin. It was not as moving as the first time they'd touched, but she was not unaffected by his hand in hers.

She looked at him, their gazes meeting and holding.

"I was thinking before you arrived that quilts are for changes in one's life, to mark it and celebrate it."

His lips curved into a very small smile. "This is hardly a new change in my life." His voice was soft enough for the words to stay just between them and deeper than it had been.

"Still, it's worth celebrating." She chose each word carefully, wanting them to be the right ones. "You told me you were your mother's child but also your own man, and I believe you. I believe that you are more than that too."

She took a careful breath, looking away from him, gathering up her thoughts.

"People have been telling me that I should be happy to be courted by you because you are a good man, because we are a good fit, and because it is time I moved on. That it is right and proper for you to court me, and that I should let you. And I will admit that there have been times when I put my own fear and hesitancies aside because I believed them. Because I thought if I pushed hard enough against that fear, I could make it go away or make it not matter."

His eyebrows were furrowed now, his mouth no longer smiling. He drew in a breath to argue or maybe apologize, but she spoke before he could.

"But I don't want that. The fact that you are a good man, or feeling like I should move on, or like I shouldn't be afraid are all terrible reasons to be with someone. I don't care if I am doing the proper thing by letting you court me. I don't care about courting at all. I never wanted to be someone's wife, and I still don't. I want to be with you because I like *you*. And I do like you, very much."

She took another long breath to steady herself, ready to take the final plunge. "You are my dearest friend. Whatever else you could be or might be to me will never be as important as that."

Now it was his turn to draw in a breath, and his eyes were dark like she'd never seen them before.

He leaned forward and she knew in that instance what his intentions were and leaned forward too.

Then he kissed her.

# Chapter 11

His mouth was hesitant against hers, just a touch of lips until she surged forward and kissed him back hard. Her hands came up to curve around his face, and her mouth pressed against his, wanting to taste and to take and to have.

His arms went around her waist, pulling them close together on the bench.

Her entire body went hot with the feel of him against her, his close, solid body, the smell of him and the taste of his mouth. She didn't even think of pausing, not now with his hands and mouth on her, not when she fancied she could feel his heart beating against her chest.

He smelled like smoke and the tang of metal and under that, just him, clean and inviting. His mouth tasted like tea and was so hot against hers, not demanding but now not afraid to take, following her lead while also coaxing her to give in return.

She wanted to devour him, to take all that he was into her until she knew him completely. She thought she'd been waiting to kiss him since the first time they'd sat like this in her workroom.

She brought one hand up to touch his cheek, the soft skin just under his ear.

He slowed the press of their mouths, tasting her over again, still not hurrying and not letting her hurry either. For all that her blood was singing in her ears, her heart beating out of control, she slowed to match him too, A slow, methodical learning of each other's touch with every press of hands and mouth, making her entire being fill, just that bit more, with joy.

They pulled away eventually, just enough space to see each other.

His eyes were questioning again, and his hands slipped from her waist, one coming up to touch his fingers to her lips.

"Is this all right?"

"Yes," she said, even though it felt like a foolish question. Hadn't she kissed him back? Hadn't she taken as much as he had? She still smiled and caught his hand before he could pull it back.

"Did you mean it? About us being friends?"

She laughed, unable to help it. "Yes, my dear, I did."

His eyes were full of wonder when he kissed her again, sliding them together until she was sitting in his lap, her arms around his shoulders, holding him close.

They drew apart again to catch their breaths and collect themselves.

"I love you," he said, his voice trembling and sweet, but there was no fear there.

There was no fear in her own mind when she answered him.

"I love you too."

# Also by EE Ottoman

Watch for more at https://eeottoman.com/.

# About the Author

EE Ottoman currently lives outside of Philadelphia with his wife and an entire house full of dogs and cats. He grew up surrounded by the farmlands and forests of upstate New York. Ottoman has an undergraduate and a graduate degree in US history and a degree in library science concentrating on archives. He is passionate about history, stories, and the queer spaces between the two. In his free time, Ottoman is an avid vegetarian cook, practicing fiber craftsperson, and novice mushroom cultivator.

Read more at https://eeottoman.com/.